The Man with the Yellowfin Tuna

The Man with the Yellowfin Tuna

Bruce Shaffer

Goathouse Publishing

Copyright © 2017 by Bruce Shaffer

All rights reserved. No part of this book may be reproduced in any manner whatsoever without written permission except in the case of brief quotations embodied in critical articles and reviews.

First Printing, 2024

All characters in this book have no existence outside the imagination of the author and have no relation to anyone bearing the same name or names. Any resemblance to individuals known or unknown to the author are purely coincidental.

Goathouse Publishing books can be ordered through booksellers or at bshaffer-forty9@gmail.com

ISBN: 979-8-8689-7340-6

DEDICATION

For my readers, without whom the pages would be blank.

ACKNOWLEDGEMENT

Thanks to my wife Karen and sons Joel and Matt for their valuable input to the story. As avid readers and terrific writers, they kept me on course. Also, thanks to my niece Kaila Sanfilippo, the exceptional artist behind the captivating book cover.

Contents

PROLOGUE: OCTOBER 1986 — 1

1 BOB'S BEETS — 5

2 DREADFUL YEARS — 24

3 A WEATHERED FACE — 57

4 DADDY'S HERE — 82

5 RIDE OF THE VALKYRIES — 106

6 A CURIOUS PASTE — 132

PROLOGUE: OCTOBER 1986

Andrea Miller is an adorable 3-year-old girl. Not the ordinary adorable, but the Shirley Temple kind of adorable, the epitome of sugar and spice and everything nice. She sits on a king-size bed with legs crossed. The sun shines through a large picture window, illuminating her dark curly hair adorned with pink ribbons. She wears a matching pink dress and black shoes.

Andrea's father, George, stuffs clothes hurriedly into a large leather suitcase resting on the bed next to her. George is 26 years-old and slender, the unnatural slender of a man who doesn't take time to eat.

His work is demanding, upwards of 80 hours a week hustling insurance. When not calling prospective clients from the office or from home; he calls them from pay phones at Andrea's gymnastics lessons, at noisy gas stations, and at busy malls.

His home life is even more demanding, an incessantly nagging wife Zanetta and an autistic son Billy. Most of the nagging is over George's reluctance to try new therapies for Billy, but some of it's over George's unruly habits, such as peeing in the shower, cracking his knuckles, and picking his ears. If ever a man needed to escape it all, George was him.

Beads of sweat dot George's stubbly face as he stuffs more clothes into the suitcase. Andrea looks confusedly at him and asks in her helium voice, "Where are we going daddy?"

"On a big adventure, just me and you."

"What about mommy and Billy?"

"Not this time, it's just us. We're gonna have so much fun. Come here my little Noodle!"

Andrea crawls to George, who tickles her and stuffs her into the suitcase. She squirms and giggles hysterically while he laughs maniacally. Andrea briefly escapes from the suitcase, only to have George pin her on her back on the bed. He picks up Andrea, still giggling hysterically, and bounces her on the bed repeatedly with both hands firmly under her arms. They collapse onto the bed in an exhausted heap. George draws a cleansing breath.

"Like I said, we're gonna have so much fun Noodle. But daddy needs to pack a few more things now, then we can start our big adventure!"

"Hurry daddy!"

George gets more clothes from the dresser and deposits them into the suitcase.

"Hurry daddy!"

"Almost done Noodle. Let me hear you count; I'll be done before you get to ten." He grabs a stack of children's books from the bookcase against the wall, including those Christmas classics, *How the Grinch Stole Christmas!* and *Rudolph the Red-Nosed Reindeer.*

"One, two . . ."

He hovers above two framed photos on the dresser. A gold-framed photo shows the Miller family, smiling on the beach in front of a spectacular sunset over the ocean. A bikini-clad Zanetta is wrapped in George's arm, and they raise tropical drinks to the camera. Andrea and Billy are plopped on the ground, tan skin sugar-coated with white sand and thick hair tousled from hard play.

A silver-framed photo shows a macho George with ballcap and shades, chest puffed and face stern, standing by a 300-pound yellowfin tuna. The fish hangs from a hook by George's head, staring at him with mouth agape, seemingly wondering how the hell this scrawny man got the best of him. George takes the tuna photo.

"Three, four . . ."

George deposits the load into the suitcase.

"Five, seven . . ."

He returns to the dresser a final time and grabs more clothes.

"Six, eight . . ."

George presses the last of the clothes into the suitcase and zips it shut. He shouts, "Done!" just as Andrea shouts, "Ten!"

"Let's go Noodle."

George carries the suitcase in one hand and leads Andrea away with the other. They go slowly down a creaky wooden staircase, with Andrea taking huge steps like a drum major at halftime. George puts down the suitcase in the small, white-tiled entryway. They turn back and look in the house one last time. Andrea shouts, "Bye mommy! Bye Billy!"

"Let's go Noodle."

George picks up the suitcase and they step out the front door into a gorgeous autumn day. Birch trees sway gently in the breeze. Leaves fall and dance on the lawn. Billowy white clouds dot a brilliant blue sky. Back in the house, pools of blood ooze from the bodies of Zanetta and Billy, who lie crumpled against the washer and dryer.

1

BOB'S BEETS

1

A pair of haggard buzzards perch on a cyclone fence; looking for an easy meal in the impoverished community of Rogersville, Texas. The fence surrounds an abandoned beet processing plant, the middle of which sprouts a drab two-story concrete building. A faded rusty sign is attached above a bank of broken glass doors at the building's entrance. Bullet holes riddle the sign, which displays a man with a beaming smile holding up a can of Bob's Beets. A construction worker with a white hardhat and an orange vest stands on a knoll overlooking the site. He puts a megaphone to his mouth. "Clear the area. Repeat, clear the area."

Others with hardhats and orange vests take their places. The construction worker blows an air horn. "Commencing countdown." He pauses, then bellows, "Three, two, one!" He pushes a red button on a remote control. The massive concrete building implodes, sending a dirty brown mush-room cloud into the sky.

2

Detective Malcolm O'Reilly, a fit gray-haired man in a suit and tie, sits at a cluttered desk sipping a steaming cup of black coffee. Nearing retirement from the Lonebud, Texas police force; Malcolm considers future endeavors. He peruses a travel brochure intently, and sets his coffee cup on the desk next to his nameplate and a calendar that shows June 2016. He crumples the brochure and tosses it through a toy basketball hoop suctioned to the wall above a garbage can. Marge, the elderly office secretary with a beehive hairdo, walks by as the brochure enters the can. "Two points," she notes.

Malcolm corrects her with a faint Irish accent. "Three, I was beyond the arc."

"And where, pray tell, is the arc?"

Malcolm smiles. "Wherever I want it to be."

"I see. Who's in the garbage can?"

"Norway. Their fjords are beautiful, but I don't know about the weather."

"You should think about going to Brazil. I went there a few years ago and had a great time— the beaches, the colonial towns, and Rio baby!" Marge does a jig.

"Rio huh? Not for me." Malcolm grabs another travel brochure and reads. "Switzerland. I do like chocolate."

"Well there ya go. I'll leave you to your studies now. Good luck Malcolm."

Marge leaves and Malcolm sets the Switzerland brochure on the desk next to a framed photo of himself with a stunning woman and a ponytailed girl. He stares at the photo and smiles.

3

A bulldozer operator moves debris into a pile at the Bob's Beets demolition site. A bright reflection from the pile catches his eye. He peers closely at the pile, dismounts the bulldozer, and walks to the reflection. He picks up a pair of brass handcuffs and kicks the surrounding dirt. A puzzling collection of blood-stained bra cups surfaces, strewn together into a morbid necklace. The bulldozer operator goes pale and can only mutter, "What the fuck?"

4

The phone rings at Malcolm's desk. Malcolm puts down an Australian travel brochure and answers. "O'Reilly. Right, be there in a sec." He hangs up and walks down the hallway to the office of Chief Orville Pritchard, an American hero and a red-blooded Texan.

You may recall the Phister Heist in the news several years ago. Two teenage punks tried to rob the Phister Piggly Wiggly. They each wielded an M249, courtesy of their careless enlisted fathers, and had all the employees and customers on the ground shitting their pants. They calmly left the Piggly Wiggly with two shopping carts full of microwave popcorn, for some massive rave they were going to throw.

Chief Pritchard, a rookie officer then, sped to the scene and confronted the punks as they loaded the last of the popcorn into their car. He ordered them to freeze and drop their weapons, but the punks jumped into the car with rifles chattering at him. He took bullets to both legs, and from a prone position took one shot at the fleeing vehicle, which was all he would need. The vehicle, a '71 Ford Pinto, burst into flames as the well-placed shot struck the gas tank. The punks suffered third-degree burns over most of their bodies, and the popcorn popped into mounds of white.

The headline of the conservative Phister Herald proclaimed, "Popcorn Justice Served," and the Piggly Wiggly even gave Officer Pritchard a lifetime supply of microwave popcorn. Officer Pritchard was well on his way up the ranks in law enforcement.

Now he directs the Lonebud Police Department as Chief Pritchard. A native Texan, he eats his steak rare, sports a waxed handlebar mustache, and speaks with a thick southern drawl. Malcolm knocks on the Chief's door. The Chief sits at his desk, face buried in papers, stroking his handlebar mustache.

"Come on in . . . sit. I got a strange one for ya Malcolm. You know that ol' beet factory they blew up last week in Rogersville? Well guess what, the demolition guys found some weird shit in the rubble. We're talkin' handcuffs, whips, and chains. But the weirdest and most troublesome thing is a necklace made of bra cups."

Malcolm's stomach pangs. "Come again?"

"A necklace made of seven torn and blood-stained bra cups, in all colors and sizes." The Chief's livid face briefly turns a deep shade of burgundy. "I sent Detective Lawson out there to investigate while you were takin' care of business."

"Oh that, my colonoscopy. It came out squeaky clean."

"Glad to hear it. Anyway, Lawson found some survivalist shit— canned food, water, batteries, and a flashlight. I think a perv was livin' there."

"In an abandoned beet factory? How could anyone live there?"

"All the shit was found in the debris from the basement. Lots of people live in basements." The Chief repositions in his chair. "And then I shut 'em down."

"Shut who down?"

"The demolition guys. Lawson found a piece of concrete rubble with 'HELP' scratched on the surface, and a large marble pestle stained green with guacamole and crimson with blood."

"I see."

"The bra cups, the rubble, the pestle; that was enough for me to suspect foul play. So I shut 'em down and sent in our boys. They didn't find any bodies. I want you to find this fuckin' squatter so we can question him. You got ten boxes of shit from the site to look through. Let's see where it leads. How's that for a retirement present?"

"I'd rather have a gold watch."

"You might just get that gold watch if I have anything to say about it."

"Thanks Chief. I'll get started looking through those boxes."

Chief Pritchard reburies his face in papers. "I got my own shit to look through."

5

Malcolm sits at a large wooden table beneath buzzing fluorescent lights in the spacious evidence room. He glances at the lights, pulls out a pair of ear plugs from his pocket, and plops them into his ears, as he's done hundreds of times over the course of his career.

Ten boxes rest on the table. After Detective Lawson's compelling discoveries, Chief Pritchard had field technicians search for and gather more items from the Bob's Beets demolition site, which now reside in the boxes. The field technicians screened the items for fingerprints. Malcolm's job is to find items of interest that the lab technician can screen for DNA. He systematically rummages through sealed plastic bags in the boxes with latex-gloved hands.

The first plastic bag contains a dented and pierced can of Bob's Beets, with Bob himself on the can, all 300 pounds of him, giving an emphatic thumbs-up sign. A viscous mixture of dirt and beet juice, like 10W-40 motor oil, pools at the bottom of the bag. Malcolm grimaces and sets the bag on the far end of the table. During the course of his work, many more undesirable bags go next to the beets.

Malcolm also finds many desirable bags, his gems. They contain clothing, books, music, toiletries, sex toys, drugs, money, and the things of which Chief Pritchard spoke— the handcuffs, whips, and chains. His brightest gems are that bizarre necklace made of blood-stained bra cups and the guacamole pestle stained with blood. He almost overlooks perhaps his brightest gem, a cheesy romance novel. Not the novel itself, but the bookmark that barely peeks out of the book. It's a torn and spotted photo of a man with a yellowfin tuna.

Hours pass and Malcolm becomes exhausted. He walks over to Sam, the security guard stationed at the door, with his box of gems. Sam sits with a perpetual smile at a small wooden table on which an open book and pen rest. "All done Sam, I got some items to check out."

"You got it, you know the drill."

Malcolm chucks his latex gloves in a garbage can and spends a minute signing the book. Sam yearns for conversation. "I hear you're gonna hang 'em up."

"Yeah, I'm tired of chasing scum each day. It's time to have some more enjoyable pursuits."

"Like what?"

"Like travel, for one."

"I hear ya. Me and the misses want to stroll down the Vegas Strip someday."

"You'll have a good time, but watch out for the beaver cards."

"Beaver cards?"

"Never mind. Gotta go over to the lab now. Always a pleasure Sam."

"Beaver cards? I'll have to look that one up."

6

Malcolm enters the forensics lab where Ted, the lab technician, is working. Ted wears a shower cap, latex gloves, goggles, and a white lab coat, and squeezes a red drop from an eyedropper into a petri dish. "Hi Ted, how's my favorite lab rat?" Malcolm is sincere; he thinks Ted looks like a rat with his beady eyes and twitchy nose.

Ted puts down the eyedropper. "Overworked and underpaid."

"Then you probably don't want these goodies from the Bob's Beets case." Malcolm holds out his box of gems.

"I was expecting you. Pritchard told me about the case, some weirdo squatter. Told me to make it a priority. Looks like another late one tonight." Ted takes the box.

"Thanks, get some sleep if you can."

"Yeah right. Tonight I'll be suckin' on the java."

7

Malcolm hopes Ted can work his magic and find conclusive DNA evidence, but that could take weeks. The same can be said of the fingerprint test results. In the meantime, Malcolm continues the investigation, which starts each morning with a steaming cup of black coffee. Occasionally he peeks at another travel brochure.

Today a crumpled brochure lies on the ground next to Malcolm's garbage can. Marge walks by, noting the errant shot. "You're losing your touch Malcolm."

"Every great athlete has a slump."

"Who's on the floor?"

"Zimbabwe."

"Thinking of going on safari?"

"Not anymore, too expensive."

The phone rings at Malcolm's desk, and he waves "bye" to Marge while answering it, "O'Reilly . . . coming Chief."

Malcolm hangs up and walks down the hallway to Chief Pritchard's office. He draws a deep breath and walks through the open office door. The Chief sits at his desk, face buried in papers, stroking his handlebar mustache. "Have a seat." Malcolm obliges. "So Malcolm, what's new in the Bob's Beets case?"

A week has passed without much progress in the case. The Chief's penetrating brown eyes feel like a double-barrel shotgun pointed in his face, but Malcolm keeps calm and answers with confidence and optimism. "Forensics is processing fingerprint and DNA evidence, but I'll keep the investigation moving forward."

"How?"

"I'll circulate high-resolution copies of the photo of the man with the yellowfin tuna to law enforcement, newspaper publishers, and television stations throughout Texas."

"Good."

"And I'll conduct interviews with people by the Bob's Beets plant. I fear there are victims out there somewhere. Why won't they come forward?"

"Maybe they can't. Better take the dogs."

8

Rogersville, Texas— population 456. Rumor has it Lana Sanders left her husband, so that would make it 455. In its heyday, the Rogersville food processing industry supported five processing plants and over 3,000 residents. Cheap Mexican labor led to the closure and abandonment of the plants, and to the demise of Rogersville. Bob's Beets was the last plant to be abandoned some 20 years ago, and it was the last to be demolished by state government, who deemed it a major eyesore.

Those who remain in Rogersville try to make a living by farming, but the arid climate makes it a tough go, and many families are on welfare. They live in trailers and double-wides, and eat what they can with food stamp purchases from the EZ-Mart.

Malcolm walks into the 10-square-block residential area of Rogersville. He's temporarily blinded by a gust that kicks up dust into his eyes. He stops to put drops in his eyes and sunglasses on his face. Tumbleweeds roll by his feet and he feels like a bowling pin. Buzzards soar overhead.

Malcolm resumes his trek. First up is the Gomez trailer. Armando Gomez answers the door and smiles, a missing-front-tooth smile. "Hola, qué tal?"

Malcolm tries his Spanish with a faint Irish accent. "Estoy bueno . . . wait . . . estoy bien. Habla inglés?"

The missing-front-tooth smile gets wider. Armando tries his English with a Hispanic accent. "A little bit."

"Good. I want to show you a picture." Malcolm takes out a copy of the tuna photo. "Have you ever seen this man?"

"That is a big fish."

Malcolm scratches his head and tries again. "El hombre, you see?" He points to his eyes and then to the man in the photo.

"That is a small man."

Malcolm loses his patience. "Shit."

"Mierda?"

Malcolm is done. "Gracias por . . . uh . . . tiempo . . . gracias por su tiempo. Adiós."

"Adiós amigo."

Next up is the Smith double-wide. Malcolm knocks and immediately hears scurrying. Dressed in a suit and tie and wearing sunglasses,

Malcolm understands that his professional attire unnerves some of the residents of Rogersville, who take a moment to tidy up before opening the door.

A faint, "Coming" sounds through the door. A few more seconds pass, and then Jenna Smith opens the door holding a crying baby. "Hi, can I help you?"

"Yes, sorry for the interruption. I'll make this quick, you have your hands full." The poopy diaper smell is overwhelming and Malcolm struggles to breathe. He takes out the copy of the tuna photo. "Have you ever seen this man?"

Jenna concentrates on the photo. "No, never."

Malcolm is overcome with stench and must leave now. "Okay, thank you ma'am. Have a wonderful day." He exits quickly and takes a deep breath, then shakes his head and mumbles, "Pointless."

9

Malcolm is tired and frustrated after traversing the 10-square-block residential area of Rogersville. He has no positive identifications of the man with the yellowfin tuna. The afternoon sun is getting low when Malcolm drives to the Bob's Beets demolition site where two Lonebud canine units, consisting of German Shepherds Crockett and Tubbs and their handlers Officers Robertson and Tyson, await in SUVs. Malcolm gets out of his vehicle to greet them. "Good afternoon officers."

"Good afternoon Detective O'Reilly," says Officer Tyson. "So, what's the deal?"

"The deal is we let the dogs out and see what happens."

"What are you expecting to find?"

"Nothing, for God's sake nothing."

The Bob's Beets demolition site is surprisingly clear after only a week of clean up before Chief Pritchard declared the site a crime scene. Sporadic mounds of concrete rubble litter the site. The omnipresent buzzards circle above in a sky turning cloudy and dark, and the persistent wind blows the tumbleweeds.

Crockett and Tubbs start their search at the center of the demolished concrete building, and systematically work their way outwards in concentric rings. Crockett trots counter-clockwise and Tubbs trots clockwise, with noses down and tongues hanging. The dogs stop and yelp wildly at a location 50 yards from where they started, and only 10 yards from where most of the Bob's Beets evidence was found.

Malcolm, Robertson, and Tyson run to the dogs. Rain starts to fall. Robertson and Tyson issue the command, "Dig!" and Crockett and Tubbs churn up dirt furiously, like a Big Bud plow on a farmer's field. After a minute of digging, the officers issue the command, "Stop!" and the dogs obey. Malcolm and the officers peer into the hole with flashlights, and Malcolm becomes nauseated by the sight of human bones.

10

Ted has several more late nights "suckin' on the java" to stay alert testing the human bones from the Bob's Beets site for DNA. Malcolm has a tough time waiting for the test results. He tosses and turns in bed at night, and his mind wanders. He worries that the perv he's chasing may also be a mass murderer. The medical examiner's preliminary determination was that the bones are relatively new, but then Malcolm reassures himself that the bones are probably those of the Comanche tribe, which has ancient burial grounds discovered frequently throughout Texas.

Malcolm's thoughts drift to his childhood in Ireland, where he excelled at hurling until a devastating knee injury. They drift to his parents who each worked two jobs to support the family, and ultimately send him to college in America. And they drift to that tragic night 25 years ago when a drunk driver killed his beloved wife and daughter.

Malcolm was a young cop then. He took a leave of absence from the police force to deal with his pain, but the pain got the best of him. Malcolm let himself go; the food binges, the excessive drinking, and the absence of personal hygiene. He barricaded himself in his house for two weeks, and would have been there longer if not for a knock on the door.

Malcolm never opened the door, but through the peephole he saw a mom and daughter selling Girl Scout cookies. He saw in them his own wife and daughter, and realized he must return to work to protect the wives and daughters and the general public; whether it's from burglars, murderers, or drunk drivers. Malcolm went to work the next day.

Now 25 years later, Malcolm still has that commitment to protect the general public. He worries about catching the Bob's Beets perv before he retires, and so he tosses and turns in bed at night, and wakes up with sweaty sheets.

11

Joe from the mailroom plops a heavy document onto Malcolm's crowded desk. "This'll keep you busy," he says. Joe catches a glimpse of Malcolm's computer monitor and smiles. "I'm sorry, looks like you're already quite busy."

Malcolm turns bright red with a monitor screen full of women in bras. "Oh this, just doin' some research." He's successfully identified two of the seven bra cups in the weird bra-cup necklace found at Bob's Beets. On the screen is a third successful identification, the Dream Angels Push-Up Bra from Victoria's Secret, retailing for a pricey $59.50.

"I want your job," says Joe as he pushes the mail cart away, still eyeing the monitor.

Malcolm delves into the massive document on his desk. It's the forensics report describing the results of the fingerprint and DNA testing of evidence from the Bob's Beets site. He spends an hour skimming it, and drains two cups of black coffee before calling Chief Pritchard. "Hi Chief, I've got some disappointing news on the Bob's Beets case, can I come over?"

A muffled, "Shit" emanates from the phone, then silence.

"Can I come over Chief?"

"Yes, of course."

"Be right there."

Malcolm continues the conversation in Chief Pritchard's office. "Dammit Chief, the forensics report says the demolition blast contaminated ninety-five percent of the evidence. Of the remaining five percent, fingerprint testing didn't find a match in the National Criminal Database or the Missing Persons Database. Nor did the DNA testing, but it did confirm that the stains on the bra-cup necklace are blood from multiple sources."

"Multiple sources. Your fear about victims seems to be true. Curious we had no hits in the databases."

"Maybe the perpetrator was never a criminal, just an upstanding family guy before turning bad and falling off the face of the earth. Maybe the victims were never reported missing. We just don't know at this point."

"I see. Any luck with the tuna photo?"

"I've sent it everywhere without results."

"To the Rangers?"

"Yes sir."

"To University Police?"

"Yes sir. Hell, I sent it to dozens of television stations, and their stories only drew a handful of crackpot phone calls."

"Did you send it to Heavy Chest Betty at KTEX?" They share a big laugh. Heavy Chest Betty is Betty Jordan, young and beautiful and well-endowed. Known for consistently doing her stories facing the camera in profile, a KTEX ratings boon.

Malcolm answers still laughing. "Yes sir. Didn't hear a word of her story, but I enjoyed it thoroughly." He composes himself. "The man in the tuna photo is wearing a ballcap and shades, making identification difficult. The Kodak photo paper dates back to the eighties, so we've tried age progression too. Could be the man now looks completely different from the photo and the age-progressed drawings. And even if the man could be identified, is he the perv or just some fisherman totally unrelated to the case?"

"My money says he's the perv. That photo makes my balls ache."

"Excuse me?"

"Some people can predict bad weather with their trick knees, I can spot deviants with my trick balls. Popcorn?"

Chief Pritchard offers Malcolm some microwave popcorn. Malcolm is so startled by the quick transition from odd claim to genuine hospitality that he can only emit a weak, "Uh, no thanks."

"Suit yourself. When will the forensics report on the bones be ready?"

"Should be soon."

"Good. A lot of our eggs seem to be in that basket. Let's hope they're not cracked."

12

Marge walks up to Malcolm's desk with a smile. "I don't see any crumpled travel brochures on the floor, you must be out of your slump."

Malcolm is engrossed in papers and doesn't look up. "Not now Marge." The smile disappears from her face and her eyebrows rise in bewilderment. She never has seen this shortness from Malcolm, but respects his request and walks away.

Malcolm is so wrapped-up in reading the forensics report on the bones from the Bob's Beets site that he hasn't even sipped his morning coffee, which is cold now. He finishes the report, and has that nauseous feeling again. Malcolm stares at the wall in thought, and rapidly taps a pencil against his desk. His thoughts turn from disgust to sorrow to anger.

He launches from his chair after a minute, and stomps over to Chief Pritchard's office. Malcolm knocks unannounced on the Chief's closed door, which is never a good idea.

A gruff, "Who is it?" comes from behind the door.

"Malcolm."

"Just a minute." And after a minute, "Come in." A coup, Malcolm has gained entry, but the Chief is not happy. "Damn, I just got off the phone with Finance. Our budget is getting reduced another two-hundred-k. You know you're irreplaceable Malcolm, and with that budget I literally don't know how I'll be able to fill your position after you retire. Shit, that's enough of my bitching. What's up?"

The Chief's question is just a formality. He can see the anger in Malcolm's eyes and knows what's up. "I read the forensics report on the bones from the Bob's Beets site; seven female victims, Chief; seven positive IDs of missing persons.

That's a victim for each of the seven bra cups in that grotesque necklace. All of them high school dropouts into drugs or prostitution."

Chief Pritchard can only whisper, "Son of a bitch."

"I think our perv was quite comfortable at the abandoned Bob's Beets plant these last twenty years, or some of them anyway. I suspect his victims would drift through town, and he'd lure them with food, money, or drugs. Once he had them in his lair, he'd keep them until he was through with them."

"How'd he kill 'em?"

"Blows to their heads; all of them had crushed skulls. Probably from the guacamole pestle. The DNA testing confirmed the pestle had blood from multiple sources."

"I don't understand, no one ever saw anything funny all those years?"

"Our perv was careful in the basement of the plant. I imagine he only left to get food and drugs, and if he was lucky he'd get a girl too."

"And no one at the—"

"EZ-Mart? No, no one at the EZ-Mart recognized the man in the tuna photo."

"Where'd he get money to buy food?"

"I think he had a large stash of money from his previous life and used it sparingly. We found over ten-thousand dollars in the rubble."

"So the bomb blast caught him off guard."

"I think so. He must not have known about the demolition crew above his secure basement. Once he regained his faculties after the blast, he probably gathered as much money as he could and made his way to the surface. The demolition guys must have quit for the day, so he was in the clear."

"He must be in bad shape."

"Our boys didn't find any trail of blood, but he might have broken bones or internal injuries. We've alerted medical facilities throughout the state."

"Where'd he get his drugs?"

"Same place as the food, at the EZ-Mart. You buy enough OTC drugs and you can get high as a dime; we're talking Nyquil, Sudafed, No Doz, Dramamine, Tylenol, Apidren, Exlax—"

"High as a dime? It's 'high as a kite', and 'stop on a dime'."

"Oh yeah," says Malcolm sheepishly.

"He must have looked and smelled like shit; didn't the EZ-Mart workers notice a regular customer like that?"

"They remember 'See-saw' Anderson and 'Jiggles' Dunbar, each with a gnarly gray beard halfway to the floor and a camembert aroma. Both of them checked out clean, so to speak. Our boy had soap and water and kept fairly clean. We didn't even find much trash in the rubble, so he must have tossed it out at various dumpsters."

"I don't understand this guy, living in the ground like that."

"He had food, shelter, and books. And he indulged in sex, drugs, and rock 'n roll; mostly eighties girl band crap like the *Go-Gos* and the *Bangles*. With his past, however dark it may be, perhaps living above ground wasn't an option."

"Damn, you're gonna have to earn your money on this one. It must be some comfort to know that soon all this shit will be behind you."

"Well, that is where shit belongs."

"Shit Malcolm, you're a fuckin' comedian! The next joke I wanna hear is about the contortions our boy makes after his lethal injection. Popcorn?"

Malcolm is blindsided again by another quick transition. "Huh?"

"Want some popcorn?"

"No thanks."

"Suit yourself. So now what?"

"We go national. We go global. We go to the FBI and the Interpol. We escalate outreach to all forms of media. We locate former employees of the EZ-Mart. We leave no stone unturned. We have to catch this guy for the unlucky seven, we just have to."

2

DREADFUL YEARS

1

Esperanza Perez lives alone in a primitive wood cabin. She checks a pile of alpaca wool in a rainbow of colors, and sees that she's low on red. The beautiful art and clothing that she creates from the wool is placed neatly in a corner of the cabin. Esperanza knits and weaves for a living, and today she's taking her crafts to market.

She packs her large backpack with intricate wall hangings, beaded pouches, flamboyant ponchos, and warm hats with earflaps and tassels. Then she puts on her own flamboyant poncho, with flaming red and yellow streaks. Esperanza straps on the large backpack, fastens her feet into black rubber sandals, and tops her head with a black bowler hat.

She's a striking young woman; with long silky black hair, crystal blue eyes, and smooth radiant skin. Her legs are strong from hauling her crafts to market three times a week at the central plaza of Valvino, a quaint village in the Chilean Andes.

She steps from her cabin into a backdrop of snow-capped mountains and volcanoes, a sky of deep blue and wispy white, a land of verdant valleys, and a culture of support and community. Acclimated to the 11,000-foot elevation, Esperanza breathes easily on the walk to Valvino, emitting regular puffs of white in the cool alpine air. She reaches Valvino in just under an hour, pausing once to wipe sweat from her brow.

Esperanza stops to watch kids play soccer on a patchy field near the central plaza, as she often does before going to market. The kids run to the worn-out ball like ants to a bread crumb, and a young boy scores a goal. The boy does a wild celebratory dance and his teammates join in the fun. Esperanza leaves with a smile on her face, as she always does.

The central plaza is alive with activity. Merchants chatter jovially as they set up their booths, hopeful of a profitable day. Esperanza sets up her booth next to booths of corn, potatoes, and quinoa. She likes it that way, without any competing craft booths nearby.

Soon a customer wanders by who's interested in a poncho. Esperanza makes the sale for 13,000 pesos after succumbing to a 2,000-peso discount during a short bargaining session. She's happy that she can buy herself a nice sea bass lunch and still have money to deposit at the bank. Two more sales after lunch add to her take, and she's ecstatic on the short walk to the bank on cobblestones.

The ecstasy turns to frustration as Esperanza waits in a long line at the bank, which often forms after the market closes. Many of the other successful merchants pack up their booths faster than her and beat her to the front of the line. She finally makes her deposit, and then walks on the cobblestones to the nearby internet café to conduct one last business transaction before heading home.

A converted brothel, the internet café has over 20 outdated computers, each with an even more outdated Windows XP operating system. The computers get lots of use despite their shortcomings, as Wi-Fi and cell phone coverage is spotty, and only the most prosperous villagers have internet connections in their homes.

Esperanza pays for 15 minutes, and takes her seat at a computer by a window. She sends an email to Conchita at the Juarez Ranch asking for a delivery of red alpaca wool. Conchita responds immediately that the wool can be delivered in two days. Satisfied with the response, Esperanza surfs the web for her remaining 10 minutes.

She watches a funny cat video, reads the 7-day weather forecast, and jots down a good-looking muffin recipe. Finally, she scrolls through international news and suddenly all blood drains from her head. Esperanza falls helplessly to the ground and lies there unconscious, with no signs of waking anytime soon.

2

It's four in the morning and Malcolm sleeps. In two hours he'll get up, if he heeds his radio alarm, and start another day of sleuthing. But an annoying phone call wakes him and starts his day early. "Hello," he answers in a sleepy voice. Malcolm hears mostly static on the line, and a faint female voice. "Hello," his sleepy voice repeats louder. Malcolm can't discern any dialogue so he hangs up. Almost immediately the phone rings again and ends with the same result, Malcolm hanging up without any conversation. He tries to go back to sleep, but his mind wanders.

Malcolm thinks about visiting Costa Rica after retirement. He wants to experience the food and culture, and see the beaches, volcanoes, tropical forests, and the wildlife. His thoughts are interrupted abruptly when the phone rings again. "Hello, who is this?" an alert and annoyed Malcolm answers.

The female voice comes through clearly this time. "My name is Esperanza Perez. I live in Chile and I saw the photo of—"

Her perfect English alerts Malcolm that this is just another crackpot phone call about the Bob's Beets case. "Listen lady, stop calling me!"

"But I know the man in the photo with a yellowfin tuna; he's my father."

"Okay, that's enough. I need to go now."

"Wait!" Esperanza speaks fast and passionately for a solid minute. Malcolm's jaw drops, and after a surge of adrenaline, his phone drops too. He scrambles hurriedly to pick it up. "Still there?" Esperanza inquires.

"Uh, yes. Dropped my phone. Please continue."

3

The early morning phone call from Esperanza rejuvenates Malcolm. He gets to the office early with his mind abuzz. Malcolm pushes aside all travel brochures and sips a steaming cup of black coffee. Chief Pritchard won't arrive for another two hours, so Malcolm has time to organize his thoughts.

The two hours pass quickly. Malcolm sends an email and leaves a phone message for Chief Pritchard. Then he jots down his thoughts on a notepad and sips more coffee. As Malcolm hoped, the Chief returns his call upon arriving to work. "Malcolm, interesting message, come on over."

"Coming Chief." Malcolm races to the Chief's office, partly from the effect of consuming three cups of coffee, but mostly from his eagerness to discuss the new developments in the Bob's Beets case. He knocks on the Chief's open door.

"Come in Malcolm. Popcorn?"

Malcolm is ready for the question this time, and he's a bit hungry. "Don't mind if I do." The Chief gets two bowls of popcorn and they harmonize crunching. Then Malcolm gets to business. "Chief, as I said in my message, we got a break in the Bob's Beets case. A lady from Chile named—"

The Chief is incredulous. "Chile?"

"Yes, Chile. A lady named Esperanza Perez phoned me this morning. She got quite a shock and keeled over when she saw the tuna photo online. She took down our number after she came to. Decided to call this morning, and insisted that she talk to the lead detective. Dispatch patched her through to me." Malcolm leans forward and continues. "Says her name used to be Andrea Miller, and the guy in the photo is her father, George Miller. And get this, says her father killed her brother and mother."

"No shit. And you believe her?"

"I do. I believe her. She was really emotional and quite convincing. We'll know soon enough if she's telling the truth about the murders. I already emailed the Miller names to the National Cold Case Database."

"Good. The NCCD is a godsend."

"And then she dropped another bomb on me. Says her father held her captive in a tunnel for fifteen years until she escaped."

"No shit . . . I'll be damned." The Chief massages his temples and ponders. "We still have some loose ends though. Like how'd she escape from her father?"

"And why didn't she go to the police sooner?" Malcolm adds.

"If the NCCD comes back supporting Es . . . what was her name again?"

"Esperanza."

"Right. If the NCCD comes back supporting Esperanza's story about the murders, then I think you better make plans to fly out to Chile to get more info. Our shitty budget will take a hit, but I think it's important to get all the facts. This murdering whack job has to be stopped."

"I always wanted to go to Chile." They harmonize crunching a final time.

4

It's a day of anticipation as Malcolm waits for an email response from the NCCD. He spends the morning writing a formal Memorandum for Record containing the notes he jotted down and the discussion he had with Chief Pritchard about the Bob's Beets case.

Then Malcolm takes Marge out to lunch at a great Chinese place just around the corner. The food is to die for, and Malcolm and Marge think they might do just that as they overindulge in Mushu Pork, Kung Pao Chicken, and Peking Duck.

Malcolm spends a good portion of the afternoon visiting the restroom, as the Tsingtao and the two pots of tea catch up to him. He passes Marge on two of his trips to the restroom, and suspects she has similar issues.

Another afternoon activity is researching Chile. Malcolm pulls out a Chilean travel brochure from his stack. He reads about Easter Island, Patagonian glaciers, and the Atacama Desert, and laments that he won't have any free time to see them if he goes.

Malcolm moves on to travel logistics. Chief Pritchard is right; at $1,200 for a roundtrip airplane ticket to Santiago, the Department's budget would take a hit. Add the cost of bus transportation to isolated Valvino, and hotel accommodations at the only place in town, and it's a small fortune.

And then it comes. Malcolm immediately opens the NCCD email and reads:

Detective O'Reilly,

Results are shown below pertaining to your inquiry of:

Miller, George

Miller, Zanetta

Miller, Andrea

Miller, William

Cold Case #834 was determined to involve the above parties as follows:

Date: October 21, 1986

Location: 321 Cortez Road

Blaine, Florida

Victims: Miller, Zanetta (wife, mother)

Age 24, lethal gunshot wound head

Miller, William (son)

Age 2, lethal gunshot wound head

Missing Persons: Miller, George (husband, father)

Age 26, brown hair/blue eyes

5 feet 9 inches, 145 pounds

Miller, Andrea (daughter)

Age 3, black hair/blue eyes

3 feet 0 inches, 30 pounds

Further details of Cold Case #834 can be obtained by contacting:

Blaine Police Department

1022 Government Drive

Blaine, Florida 15295

358-555-5890

Jessup County Sheriff Department

7356 Lakeport Boulevard

Farley, Florida 15284

358-555-2948

Sincerely,

NCCD staff

683-555-8372

"Alright then," says Malcolm. He closes the message and goes online to book a roundtrip airplane ticket to Santiago.

5

Twice in his long and fulfilling life Malcolm has felt near death. The first time was as a kid in Ireland when he hopped into an elevator at the department store to kill time while his parents shopped for a vacuum cleaner. He rode up alone, and the elevator became stuck between the third and fourth floors when the power went out. No backup power kicked in, and all Malcolm could do was push the alarm button and hope. He cried alone in the dark without ventilation. Rescuers couldn't get to him, but after over an hour power was finally restored and he darted out of the elevator onto the fourth floor.

The second time was on vacation in the Caribbean when his scuba tank failed on an excursion to see and swim with tropical fish. Malcolm was climbing down a rope ladder attached to the outfitter's boat, and at a depth of about 10 feet his air flow stopped suddenly. Malcolm's eyes got big and he instinctively started climbing back to the boat with no air in his lungs.

Wearing a weight belt and a heavy scuba tank, Malcolm wouldn't have made it on his own. But the dive master was watching him and the other novice divers descend, and swam quickly to Malcolm to give him his spare regulator. He grabbed it, filled his lungs, climbed to the boat, and called it a day.

Today on the bus ride to Valvino, Malcolm felt near death for the third time in his life. The ride from Santiago climbs almost 10,000 feet, along narrow, deteriorating, winding roads. Guardrails don't exist, but severe drops down the mountainside do. The bus driver sped along in driving sleet and rain, as if late for his own wedding. But here Malcolm sits in the room of his surprisingly nice Hotel Abrego, an hour early and settling his nerves with several stiff ones.

6

Esperanza steps from her cabin into an ocean of nothingness. The fog whitewashes the pervasive beauty of the Chilean Andes, and the heavy air mutes the thumping of her footsteps against the dirt trail to Valvino. She walks purposefully, bundled in her flaming red and yellow wool poncho and a warm wool hat with earflaps and tassels.

Esperanza reaches Valvino and stops to watch the kids play soccer in the fog on the patchy field near the central plaza. They have fun sloshing and slipping on the wet and muddy turf, ignoring the cold. Three of them tangle and fall going for the worn-out ball, letting out elated screams as they slide in the mud. Esperanza leaves with a smile on her face, as she always does.

She goes to the nearby Café Cabra where Malcolm is waiting. He sips a steaming cup of black coffee at a small table in the corner. The coffee is much better than Texas coffee, and is a good remedy for his mild hangover. Esperanza walks to his table. "Detective O'Reilly? I'm Esperanza."

Malcolm stands up and they shake hands. "Pleased to meet you Esperanza." And he is. He's pleased to see a pretty face, unlike the drab faces of Marge, Pritchard, and the others back at the office.

They sit down and the proprietor, Manuela, comes for Esperanza's order, which she places in perfect Spanish.

She switches to English to address Malcolm. "Welcome to Valvino. They call it the 'Pearl of the Andes'."

"Thank you. I'm sure it is, but the fog isn't letting me see much of it."

"We live in the clouds, and we live peacefully."

Manuela smiles and sets a cup of hot tea on the table. "I'm sure you do," says Malcolm. "From our phone conversation, I understand that you didn't live so peacefully before you came here. Are you prepared to talk about that?"

Esperanza sips her tea and takes a deep breath. "Okay."

"I can't thank you enough. Without your statement we may never find your father. We checked him out, and indeed he's been missing since your brother and mother were killed."

"And you suspect him of killing people at that Bob's Beets place?"

"Yes. And we suspect he sexually abused them before he killed them." Tears well-up in Esperanza's eyes. Malcolm recklessly delves further. "When you were held captive did he—" Malcolm has no need to finish the question as Esperanza breaks down. He offers a tissue and she takes it and dabs her eyes.

Soon the crying stops and Esperanza is able to speak. "I'm sorry."

"No, no, I'm sorry. We can talk about that when you're ready."

"I'm ready"

"You sure?"

"I'm sure. We need to find the bastard."

Malcolm nods, noting the intensity of her face. "We will. I need some air, how 'bout we go for a walk. Let's go see this pearl town of yours."

They take final sips of coffee and tea. Malcolm raises his hand and Manuela comes over. "La cuesta por favor," he says.

Manuela frowns with confusion. Esperanza laughs and intervenes. "Mi amigo está intentando, Manuela. El cheque por favor."

Manuela smiles and says, "Claro," then retreats to the counter by the cash register to get the check.

7

Malcolm and Esperanza do a slow lap around the central plaza, mindful of the slippery cobblestones and some puddles in their way. They stroll through the fog, which has dissipated a bit to reveal some of the snow-capped Andes peaks and the sights of Valvino. Esperanza points out the Spanish colonial church, the modest 3-tiered fountain, and the aged bronze statue of the conquistador Pedro de Valdivia.

The market is closed today and the plaza is quiet, except for the distant chatter of the kids playing soccer. The quiet is conducive to an extended conversation, which Malcolm instigates when he sits at a bench overlooking the Andes. "Gorgeous . . . you do have a pearl here. In my town we have cows and chickens."

Esperanza laughs and joins him on the bench. "I'm sure you have some nice things; maybe a nice family?"

Esperanza is fooled by the wedding ring that Malcolm still wears. "Not anymore. I'll tell you about that another time. Right now I'd like to talk about you, and I'd like to record our conversation. Is that okay?"

Esperanza nods.

"Thank you." Malcolm takes out a digital voice recorder and starts it. "Alright then, I have to ask how you recognized that tuna photo. It was taken so long ago."

"I could never forget that photo. Billy and I used to hop into bed with mom and dad and cuddle. I felt so happy and loved. You don't forget that feeling. I'd fall asleep with that feeling, looking at the photo just a few feet away on the dresser." Esperanza's disposition changes. "Later I despised that photo, when it was just a few feet away in that hell hole he kept me in for fifteen years. No, I could never forget that photo."

"Why didn't you go to the police sooner, after you escaped?"

"I was afraid. He told me never to tell anyone about the killings or I'd be next. I believed him. He's psycho. It's very peaceful here in Valvino, but I live in fear and always have an eye on my back. As for the abuse, I was too ashamed to tell the police. The things he did, I couldn't tell them."

"Why did you call me that night, and why are you speaking with me now?"

"My heart sank when I read the story about the seven girls who were killed at Bob's Beets. Maybe that wouldn't have happened if I'd gone to the police sooner. I'll have to live with that." Esperanza dabs her eyes with the tissue. "I may always have an eye on my back, but I have an eye on the future too. A future where George Miller is dead or behind bars, and women won't have to live in fear anymore."

Malcolm stops the digital voice recorder. "I have just a few more questions, but first I think we should do another lap."

"Yes, another lap. Let's go."

8

Malcolm and Esperanza do another slow lap around the central plaza. The fog has lifted and the sun shines down on them. They stretch to the heavens to absorb as much of it as they can. The plaza remains quiet, and the distant chatter of the kids playing soccer has ceased. They return to their bench rejuvenated, and continue their conversation. Esperanza surprises Malcolm with a question. "Do you like the *Bangles?*"

"The who?"

"Not the *Who*, the *Bangles.*"

"I know not the *Who*." Malcolm smiles, realizing what's happening. "This sounds like Abbott and Costello."

"Who?"

Malcolm busts out laughing. Esperanza laughs too, but she's not entirely sure why. "What was the question?

"Do you like the *Bangles?*"

"I don't know the *Bangles.*"

"The *Bangles* were a girl band from the eighties. I had to listen to them in that tunnel practically every day for fifteen years. I hate the *Bangles.*"

Malcolm takes out the digital voice recorder again and starts it. "Tell me about the tunnel, what was it like in there?" Esperanza launches into a long monologue about those dreadful years in the tunnel . . .

9

Those dreadful years in the tunnel, 15 of them by Esperanza's unmistakable count. Unmistakable because only on her birthday was she excused from her demeaning and horrific duties for her father, and she remembered every birthday. That's all she wanted to remember.

Initially the isolated tunnel in the Chilean Andes was exciting to Andrea, as she was known then. As a 3-year-old on an adventure with her daddy, living in the ground was fascinating, kind of like an extended camping trip.

As Andrea got older, the camping trip lost its luster. Andrea was given more chores to do, and her father began touching her where she had never been touched before. By the time Andrea reached puberty she was confused and miserable. Her father said the bleeding from her period and the other changes to her body were God's punishment for not always doing as he said.

Andrea's life as a teenager was hell. Sometimes she tried to escape when her father was drug-impaired, but he was able to catch her each time and her hell persisted. She had to give her father sponge baths, and scrub vigorously between his legs. She had to cook and do the dishes, every meal on every day except her birthday. And she had to do the laundry, the worst of which was her father's underwear often with shit, piss, or semen stains.

Andrea had to frequently carry out the actual shit and piss in buckets, and dump them in the nearby bushes. To prevent escape during sewage disposal and overnight sleeping, she wore a long chain around her ankle that was tethered to a fixed pole in the tunnel.

Even worse was being handcuffed to the pole for up to two days when her father left to dump garbage and buy supplies. He'd buy food, water, drugs, books, and magazines at a small but well-stocked market a dozen miles away at the intersection of two narrow dirt roads. When he returned, Andrea would be sitting in her own excrement, hungry, thirsty, and weeping.

Andrea's father considered all forms of media to be sacred. Every day she had to dust off the cassette player and tapes, the shortwave radio, and the books and magazines, which was futile in a dirt tunnel.

Andrea despised the music and the shortwave radio. Such hits as *We Got the Beat* and *Walk Like an Egyptian* rocked the tunnel constantly and pounded in her head endlessly. Her father broadcast the shortwave throughout the world, and Andrea could only listen helplessly with duct tape over her mouth, longing for the day when she could see the world.

Most of the books and magazines were in Spanish, which her father could read since the Miller household was bilingual, a byproduct of his Chilean wife. He met and fell in love with Zanetta while in the Peace Corps, teaching entrepreneurs and small business owners how to develop and market their products throughout Chile.

Andrea could read the Spanish books and magazines too, and they were her salvation. For about a week each month she read by the moonlight that filtered through the opening in the tunnel while her father slept, being sure to return the literature to its exact location. Turning on the flashlight to read was out of the question, since it was kept by his side at night to investigate any strange noises.

Andrea's reading ability wasn't great, but she persisted and eventually it was good enough to learn. She learned all kinds of things about life, including two very tangible facts— she hadn't been punished by God, but had experienced puberty; and she wasn't being loved, but was being sexually assaulted.

Andrea's evolving knowledge was her strength, and she began to have hope. So she called herself Esperanza, which she had learned meant "hope," even if her father still called her Noodle or Bitch.

10

Malcolm is dumbfounded by what he's heard and can only shake his head. Eventually words come. "I'm so sorry. No one deserves that."

Esperanza dabs her eyes with the tissue and blows her nose. A young boy of seven limps up to them with a club foot. His pleading eyes sparkle. "Chiclets?" he asks. Esperanza cannot resist. She grabs a couple of boxes from the boy's tray and pays him 1,000 pesos. His face lights up and he gives her a big hug before limping away.

Esperanza's tears are gone now and she smiles. "I don't dwell on the past. I enjoy what I do now. I make decent money and I support my people whenever I can."

"I can see that."

Esperanza pops a Chiclet into her mouth and gives Malcolm one. He chews and ponders. "How'd you do it? How'd you manage to escape?"

"How'd I escape? Let me tell you . . ."

11

By 16 Esperanza had blossomed into a beautiful young woman and the sex became more frequent. Inevitably she became pregnant, and she knew she must escape for the baby's sake as well as hers. She devised a plan.

The plan involved getting pills for morning sickness. Esperanza didn't have morning sickness, but she mustered up a few nasty vomits by drinking salt water to convince her father that she did. He got the pills on an excursion for supplies, and kept them locked up in a wooden box with his own stash of drugs.

Each morning her father gave her two capsules, not wanting anymore nasty vomit odors permeating the tunnel. Esperanza pretended to take the capsules with a glass of water, but secretly removed them from her mouth and put them in her pocket. She removed the powder from the capsules while she was cooking, and put the powder in an empty pill bottle that her father had thrown away. Esperanza hid the bottle in a bag of flour, where it was safe since her father never cooked. Gradually the bottle filled, until the time was right to empty it.

The right time came 15 years overdue, on a dark night under a new moon. The darkness appealed to Esperanza for concealment, in case somehow her father wasn't knocked on his ass and could chase after her.

She served him the usual evening tea, but spiked it with the powder of 40 morning sickness pills. Esperanza masked any funny taste with lots of sugar, just the way he liked it.

He was loopy within 15 minutes of draining his cup, and nearly comatose within 30. Esperanza calmly put on her jacket, filled the pockets with snacks, and grabbed the flashlight and the shortwave. She hovered over her father contemplating a violent act, but settled on a gentle kick. He didn't budge; it was time to go.

Clouds moved in during the first mile of Esperanza's journey to freedom, and a full-blown storm had developed by mile three. The relentless wind and rain pelted her face, and she ditched the shortwave which was heavy and soaked beyond repair.

Periodic flashes of lightning illuminated her path and rumbles of thunder shook the ground. One flash illuminated a surreal curved and twisted mountain peak pointing high into the sky. Esperanza was pregnant, cold, exhausted, and afraid, but somehow gravity helped pull her down the rocky mountainside.

She reached a small brook at dawn and slept under a majestic poplar tree until noon. The storm had passed and the sun peeked from the clouds, beaming a ray onto her face. A face with a faint smile, and a head filled with dreams of a happy new life.

12

Malcolm is impressed. "Amazing. You're a resourceful girl. I'm glad you made it out. I'm glad we have this day together."

"I only wish those pills were stronger."

Esperanza pops another Chiclet into her mouth and gives Malcolm another one. "Thanks," he says. "The flavor in these buggers doesn't last very long, does it?"

Esperanza smiles, a smile Malcolm wishes he saw more. "No, but that's okay. Gives our Chiclet peddlers some job security."

"Here, here. I used to peddle candles as a boy in Ireland."

"Really? You don't seem like the candle type."

"I'll have to tell you about it another time." Malcolm holds up the digital voice recorder. "Wouldn't want to record my deepest secrets." He chews and ponders. "How'd you end up in Valvino?"

"Pure chance. I wandered into the small mining town of Pichipunto. An old couple took me in for the night, seeing that I was cold, wet, and pregnant. They fed me a hot meal and I took a hot shower, and the next morning I left. I knew I had to get much further away from the tunnel, so I hitch-hiked. I hopped from vehicle to vehicle for two days. My last ride was in a truck delivering water to a cistern in Valvino."

"Then what? Where'd you stay?"

"Then Paola Ramos, God rest her soul."

"Who?"

"Paola Ramos. She took me under her wing. I was safe with her at her tiny place just up the road. She had a few alpacas and spun her own wool. Taught me everything I know about knitting and weaving."

"I love your hat. Did you make that?"

Esperanza smiles and fiddles with the tassels on her hat. "Yeah, I sell them at the market three times a week. Paola used to take me there when she sold her crafts. Showed me everything about the business— displaying crafts, bargaining, restocking supplies—"

"Avoiding Carpal Tunnel Syndrome?"

"Ha ha. Actually, I find making things therapeutic, not a strain on my hands. So that's what I do."

"Where's your shop?"

"I work in my home. After Paola died I built my own little cabin a few miles north of here."

"You ARE a resourceful girl."

"It gets a bit cramped with all of my supplies, but I can step out into my front yard and view the vast Andes."

"My front yard has a view of my neighbor's front yard." Malcolm shakes his head in disgust. "Well, that's all for now. Thank you Esperanza." He stops the digital voice recorder. "One more thing though. I'll need to corroborate your information. How 'bout we go find a tunnel?"

13

Pichipunto is a small mining town. You may recall the trapped miners that were rescued there a few years ago. A portion of the mine collapsed while the miners were digging for copper, leaving them trapped some 2,000 feet underground for over 50 days. Their rescue attracted world attention, and Broadway even made a play about the disaster.

When not making world news, Pichipunto is a quiet town where the locals enjoy rodeos, cookouts, or simply flying kites. Malcolm and Esperanza are in Pichipunto, not to enjoy any of these activities, but to begin their search for Esperanza's dreadful tunnel.

Chief Pritchard approved Malcolm's request to fund the search, which includes compensating Esperanza for missing sale opportunities at the Valvino market. The Chief wasn't happy about yet another hit to the Department's budget, but any evidence that they find might be invaluable to prosecute George Miller for years of sexual abuse and false imprisonment.

Malcolm and Esperanza step off a muddy bus in Pichipunto after the rigorous 12-hour ride from Valvino, each carrying a large backpack. They wave to the bus driver and set out on their quest.

Malcolm is able to keep up with Esperanza, some 30 years his junior and in much better shape, as the weather is cool and the terrain is level. By late afternoon they find the majestic poplar tree by the small brook where Esperanza rested that fateful day years ago. Malcolm chucks his backpack to the ground unceremoniously. "Whew, let's call it a day, shall we?" He grabs a water bottle from his backpack and drinks.

Esperanza sets her backpack on the ground. "Alright, let's rest. Tomorrow's going to be a long day of hiking steep terrain."

Malcolm and Esperanza set up camp. They pitch their pup tents under the poplar tree and shove their backpacks inside. Esperanza gets a bag of dehydrated stew from her tent while Malcolm digs a crude fire pit with a trowel. Suddenly he spikes the trowel in the loamy soil and barks, "Wait, put that bag of crap away!"

"But I'm starved."

"We can have the best dinner ever. I saw some brown trout jumping when we were walking along the stream."

"How are you going to catch a brown trout?"

Malcolm goes to his tent and retrieves a collapsible fly-fishing rod and a fly box. "Voilà! I fish a lot back home on the Guadalupe River. I was hoping to sneak in some fishing while I was here. Know how to fish?"

"We don't do much fishing in Valvino."

"Let me show you." Malcolm leads Esperanza slowly down the steep stream bank to solid footing at water's edge just upstream of a dead tree in the stream. He browses through the fly box. "Let's try this one." Malcolm pulls out a furry black nymph. "Now let's tie it on." He knots it to the leader, and then knots the leader to the fishing line. Then he assembles the fly-fishing rod and prepares to cast.

"Better step over here. Wouldn't want to hook you on my backswing." Esperanza moves over. "Here goes nothing." Malcolm casts the nymph into the current and lets it drift near the dead tree. "We want the nymph to sink near the streambed to get those trout interested. And a little tug on the line doesn't hurt either." He pulls up on the rod a few times but doesn't get any bites, and reels in the line after it goes too far downstream. "You try."

"I don't think so."

"Come on, it's like tossing a baseball."

"I never tossed a baseball."

"Oh. I'll show you." Esperanza grabs the rod hesitantly and Malcolm adjusts her grip. Then he grips the rod too and they cast the nymph awkwardly. They laugh after the nymph lands only five feet away. "We can do better," says Malcolm. They do it again with marginally better results. After a few better attempts Malcolm declares, "Okay, it's all you this time."

"You sure? I don't want to maim you."

"Don't worry, I'll stand clear." Esperanza launches a decent cast upstream of the dead tree and pulls up on the rod a few times. She gets no bites and reels in the line. "Nice try, keep going," says Malcolm. Esperanza launches another cast and again gets no bites. Malcolm prods jokingly, "It's getting dark, we're gonna need that fish soon."

And then a miracle happens on the third cast, a fish bites. Esperanza screams and Malcolm screams back, "Hold on!

Pull!" He runs over to grab the rod and reels in a 2-pound brown trout after a brief fight. Esperanza runs away from the fish flopping on the ground and Malcolm chuckles. He unhooks the nymph and announces, "Dinner is served."

14

Malcolm wields a pocketknife and guts the brown trout with the precision of a surgeon. Esperanza looks on as he tosses the head, intestines, heart, and other organs into the stream. She's not totally disgusted by this, having seen pigs butchered on ranches in Chile, but watching Malcolm season the gutted trout with lemon pepper is much more amenable to her eyes.

The deadwood that they gathered by the stream crackles with flame in the fire pit, imparting a sizzle to the trout in its foil container. Soon they enjoy the fruits of their labor sitting by a toasty fire— plates of steaming trout, reconstituted mashed potatoes, and cherry-flavored water. Their eager mouths chew rapidly and they swallow contentedly. Malcolm boasts, "Like I said, the best dinner ever."

"I'll give you good, but the best ever? I don't think so. We'd need a nice bottle of wine."

"I suppose you're right. This water is all we have, cheers." Malcolm raises his water bottle and Esperanza clangs it with her own. He notes, "This is nice— good food, good company, and sparkling stars blanketing the night sky."

They tip back their heads and enjoy the heavens. Malcolm reveals, "Whenever I camp I gaze up and try to spot Gemini, the twins. My wife and daughter were both Geminis, and they practically looked like twins." He adds solemnly, "But I lost them to a drunk driver in a car crash."

"That's terrible, I'm so sorry."

"I met my wife Helen at a bowling alley of all places. I was eating a burger at the greasy alley café, watching her cute body gyrations while she bowled. It was love at first sight. I struck up a conversation with her when she came to order her own burger. We were married a year later." Malcolm pauses to chew on a bite of trout. "Soon we had Ellen. She was an absolute angel. I'd come home from a hard day of work and she'd melt my heart. One look at her sweet face, or at that goofy buck-tooth gopher face she made, and all was right with the world."

Esperanza smiles. "She sounds adorable." The smile fades. "Unfortunately, we both know too well that all is not right with the world. And now you're an orphan like me."

"I guess I am somewhat of an orphan."

Malcolm points to the sky. "Look, there's Gemini. Those two bright stars are the heads of the twins. See them?"

Esperanza leans over to follow his pointed finger. "I do!"

"I get some comfort knowing they're always up there shining down on me."

Malcolm and Esperanza converse easily late into the night. The fire becomes small and the air becomes chilled. Their bellies are content and exhaustion creeps in. Malcolm yawns. "Sounds like we have a tough day of hiking tomorrow. I better hit it."

"Me too. Thanks for the fishing lesson and the wonderful dinner."

"Of course." Malcolm stands up slowly and works out the kinks after hours of sitting. "I can't believe you caught one on your third try, you're a natural!" He raises his hand and

Esperanza high-fives it. Then, after an awkward pause, they smile and hug.

"Well goodnight," says Esperanza.

"Goodnight," says Malcolm.

Esperanza walks into her tent and zips it shut. Safely alone now, Malcolm pees on the fire to put it out, and then retires to his tent for the night.

15

After a hearty breakfast of oatmeal and coffee, Malcolm and Esperanza hit the trail again in search of Esperanza's dreadful tunnel. Unfortunately for them the trail is not well-defined. It's defined only in Esperanza's fading memory of her escape under duress, on a dark and stormy night years ago.

When they come to a fork in the road, they pick a tine. When they come to a churning creek, they ford it. When they come to an impassable crag, they turn back. They begin to feel like lab rats in a maze, and start to wonder if they'll ever be rewarded in this cruelest of labyrinths. Perhaps finding the tunnel is as unlikely as finding the proverbial white cat in a snowstorm.

The pair hike for hours, climb thousands of feet, and consume buckets of water after filtering it from creeks. Malcolm falls a good 100 yards behind Esperanza, as the altitude and steep terrain begin to wear on him. Recognizing his slower pace, Esperanza drops her backpack to the ground and sits on a boulder to wait for Malcolm. Soon Malcolm discards his backpack and joins her on the boulder. "Whew, my legs are shot. You could at least pretend to be tired."

Esperanza chuckles. "I have the legs and lungs of a Valvinian. We walk for miles to market, and we're acclimated to the altitude."

"That explains it. I'm acclimated to drinking beer and watching football on my couch."

She chuckles again, a soothing sound amidst his pain; the physical pain in his legs and lungs, but mostly the mental pain in knowing it all happens again tomorrow when their quest resumes. Malcolm turns to more pressing matters. "The way I see it, we have plenty of safe water to drink using our water filters. And we have enough food to last another four days, barring any more fishing miracles. That's two more days to find the damn tunnel, and two days to get back."

"Sounds reasonable."

"I just need my body to cooperate, which starts with lots of rest. Do you mind if we stop for the day?"

"Not at all. Probably have only another hour of light left anyway."

"Good, let's set up camp."

Malcolm and Esperanza pitch their pup tents with difficulty in a steady wind. The nylon tent fabric flaps wildly and the rod connectors rattle violently. Halfway erected, Malcolm's tent collapses and starts to roll away, like those Rogersville tumbleweeds. Instinctively Malcolm dives and grabs the tent. It's a great dive, like Rickey Henderson going into second base. Esperanza finds this quite amusing and can barely say, "Are you alright?"

"I think so."

But in fact Malcolm has a spot of blood on his nose. "Wait a second, you're hurt," says Esperanza. Malcolm dabs at his nose. "I'm getting you a bandage." Esperanza digs out a first-aid kit from her backpack while Malcolm gets to his feet. She applies a bandage to his red nose, which is reminiscent of a certain reindeer. "There ya go Rudolph, or do you prefer Rudy?"

Malcolm laughs, and is touched by her concern for him. "Funny girl. Call me whatever you like."

The wind dies down and Malcolm's tent goes up. Satisfied with his abode, Malcolm pulls out his bag of dehydrated stew and a small propane stove from his backpack. Esperanza joins him at the stove with her own bag of stew.

They can't have a wonderful fish dinner tonight, or a crackling fire to warm themselves, as their campsite is void of a stream and deadwood. The campsite isn't very hospitable; dusted only with volcanic ash and spotted with rocks, grass, shrubs, and cacti.

The bland stew is not particularly satisfying, but it warms and fills their bellies. The conversation is more satisfying, especially to Malcolm. Gemini shines down on them. "I'm going to retire soon," says Malcolm. "By my count I've got thirty-nine more days of work left."

"That's great. What'll you do with all your free time?"

"Oh I've got a list of things to do. Travel's at the top. Think I'll head down to Costa Rica for a while."

"I'd love to go to Costa Rica; they have two coastlines. I haven't been to a beach since I was a little kid. I vaguely remember playing in white sand with my brother Billy."

"Plenty of beaches to choose from, that's for sure. And—"

A rare herd of chinchillas interrupts Malcolm's train of thought. They wander searching for food, with their big eyes and ears, bushy tails, and long whiskers. "How cute," whispers Esperanza. The chinchillas briefly stop and stare at them, then continue their trek. "I want one of those," she adds.

"You can get one at a fur store."

"That's not what I had in mind!"

Malcolm gets the desired result and laughs. "I know, sorry."

He recites fun things to do in Costa Rica which he's gleaned from a travel brochure, like kayaking through lush mangrove estuaries, touring a chocolate or coffee plantation, and visiting the active Arenal Volcano. Esperanza is engrossed in the conversation and hours pass. Eventually she yawns. Malcolm succumbs to the powerful contagion and yawns too. "That's enough babbling for one night. Thanks for listening. Tomorrow we find your tunnel. Good night Esperanza."

"Good night Rudy. I hope you're right about finding the tunnel tomorrow. An extra day looking for it in the Andes would be quite taxing."

"Especially on geezers like me."

And with that, Malcolm walks gingerly to his tent and zips it shut. He spends a full 15 minutes changing into his sleeping clothes, which includes peeling blood-and-dirt-stained socks from his feet, each with a nickel-sized blister on the big toe. He climbs into his sleeping bag and instantly falls asleep, the sleep of a beat man.

16

Malcolm awakens but struggles to get up. He aches everywhere, even where aches should not be. His bellybutton is sore to the touch. It's not red or abraded mind you, but nonetheless it's sore. He knows his throbbing legs must transport him to Esperanza's tunnel, not a body bag which, the way he feels, seems like a much more appropriate mode of transportation.

Malcolm becomes somewhat rejuvenated after another breakfast of oatmeal and coffee, and he and Esperanza start walking again. Up. And up. Up undefined steep rocky inclines. Sharp pain reverberates through Malcolm's feet with each step on his blisters, but eventually he becomes numb to the pain.

Esperanza has her eyes on Malcolm, and doesn't let him fall too far behind. She takes frequent breaks to let him regain his breath and rest his aching body. After hiking a mere three miles all morning they're finally rewarded. Esperanza shoots out her index finger. "Look, it's Mount Crumpit!" Indeed, it's that surreal curved and twisted mountain peak pointing high into the sky that Esperanza glimpsed during a flash of lightning on that fateful night years ago. There can be no mistaking this weathered geologic wonder for any other in the Andes.

"Say again?"

"It's Mount Crumpit, or at least that's what I call it. I saw this mountain peak when I escaped from the tunnel. We're getting close!"

"I'll drink to that." An exhausted and relieved Malcolm extends his water bottle to Esperanza, who clangs it with her own. They drink, and soon they attack the mountain with a renewed vigor that only adrenaline can give. They see the finish line to this marathon, and are going for gold.

In a half mile Esperanza provides the color commentary, "I remember this clearing." And a half mile further, "Yes, yes, this gully was here. Come on Rudy, we're almost there!"

She has a peculiar déjà vu uneasiness in her stomach, much worse than the uneasiness of a first date. Like the one she had with Jaime Morales, who rambled on about his mom and ex-girlfriend throughout dinner.

Esperanza crosses the gully, which luckily only trickles. Malcolm slips and stumbles stepping out of the gully, but deftly touches a hand to the ground and maintains his balance. "Nice save," says Esperanza with a hint of laughter.

"Just shoot me now," says Malcolm with a hint of sincerity. They plod along. Malcolm stumbles again a few hundred yards ahead, and falls down this time. "Okay, really, just shoot me now," a disgusted Malcolm demands.

"You found it!" shouts Esperanza.

"Found what? Another way to injure and humiliate myself? I'm beginning to feel like a punching bag." And indeed Malcolm has a new scrape on his forehead.

"You found the tunnel! Look around you, the ground is sunken. It shouldn't be that way, unless some dirt and rocks were removed."

"Nice detective work. We could use you back in Texas."

Malcolm and Esperanza poke around the area and find the pile of dirt and rocks from the original tunnel excavation. They investigate further, digging and removing rocks from the sunken ground with Malcolm's trowel and a small spade and pick that he brought. The digging becomes more frantic as daylight begins to fade. Then what sounds like a bell rings loudly after Esperanza jabs the spade. "What's that?" she asks. She digs some more. "My God, it's the pole!"

"Pole?"

"The pole he handcuffed and chained me to." Esperanza shudders and Malcolm offers her a comforting arm, which she accepts.

"Alright then, I'll take some pictures and record our coordinates. Forensic specialists from Texas and the FBI will want to excavate all evidence to build a case against your father."

"He's no father of mine, he's a twisted rapist and murderer."

"I know. We'll get him. Hundreds of competent law enforcement officers want him as badly as us. But now our work here is done. Tomorrow we go home."

Malcolm and Esperanza clear rocks from where they intend to pitch their pup tents a final time. An unusually sharp rock cuts Malcolm's hand as he tosses it aside. "You've got to be fuckin' kidding me!"

17

Malcolm's aches and wounds healed quickly, and he was pain-free for his retirement party. His colleagues at the Lonebud Police Department sent him out in style with a dim sum lunch at the Golden Panda House. Servers rolled food carts relentlessly, and the 100 attendees succumbed to the cornucopia of wonderful bite-sized foods. They overindulged in such delicacies as pork baos, chicken dumplings, prawn rice noodle rolls, and egg tart dessert. And they downright abused the alcohol from the open bar. No fewer than five people prayed to the porcelain gods, and another two didn't make it that far.

Marge assembled a touching slide show of Malcolm's career with the Department. It included slides of a long-haired Malcolm receiving his badge, a laughing Malcolm in the gunny sack race at the Department picnic, and a solemn Malcolm speaking at a fallen comrade's funeral.

Chief Pritchard did get that gold watch for Malcolm, who graciously accepted it, reflected on his career, and said his farewells. Few eyes remained dry following his remarks.

3

A WEATHERED FACE

1

Eight months later Malcolm enjoys the retired life in Costa Rica. His 2-week vacation there was so enjoyable that he investigated the practicality of living there permanently and he concluded, like many other Americans, that Costa Rica is a wonderful place to live. It boasts an abundance of fun outdoor, cultural, and sports activities, a low crime rate and cost of living, a tropical climate, great healthcare, attractive real estate opportunities, and English newspapers and services.

So Malcolm packed his bags and bought a modern 2-bedroom house on a 10-acre plot of land featuring tropical fruit trees, hardwood trees, a tropical garden, a vegetable garden, and a large irrigation pond. He spends his days tending the land, and his nights reading Agatha Christie mystery novels.

Twice a week Malcolm walks down to the tennis club and has a game with Pablo. Pablo usually dominates, but Malcolm enjoys running and sliding on the clay, the cold beer afterwards, and the camaraderie of club members.

Malcolm also has a Spanish lesson twice a week. His tutor is stern but effective. Just last week Malcolm was able to order lunch completely in Spanish at a local taqueria. He even made a little Spanish chitchat with the teenage server and successfully received the check on the first try.

Every morning Malcolm takes his golden retriever, Gemini, down to the beach for a game of fetch. When Gemini is exhausted, after what seems like an eternity, they both jump in the ocean to cool off and splash around.

Overall it's a good life, much better than chasing scum each day. But nights can be quiet, a little too quiet, and Malcolm fights loneliness. He's comforted by writing letters to friends back in Texas, and to his new friend in Chile:

Dear Esperanza,

I recovered nicely from my various ailments on our adventure in the Andes. I felt like such a buffoon, but I guess a few mishaps can be expected when you get to be my age. I thoroughly enjoyed our time together, even in such trying conditions.

I live in Costa Rica now after retiring eight months ago. I have a nice place here where I grow fruits and vegetables. You would be proud of me; I take my produce to market once a week and actually make a little money, which helps supplement my police pension. I hope you're selling lots of your fine wool crafts at the Valvino market.

I heard from my former police chief, and I'm sorry to say that law enforcement hasn't made much progress on the apprehension of George Miller. The forensics specialists obtained a great deal of evidence from the tunnel that we found. It will be quite useful to the prosecution when we do catch the bastard, but it hasn't helped us get any closer to catching him yet.

I hope all is well in the "Pearl of the Andes." Stay in touch and I hope we can get together again sometime. Remember, we have lots of beaches here for you!

Sincerely,
Malcolm

2

Malcolm is happy to get a reply from Esperanza two weeks later:

Dear Rudy,

Good to hear from you, and I'm glad you're feeling well. You shouldn't feel bad about your mishaps on our trek; I had a few of my own, but I was quick to get up when you weren't looking. Your stamina in that altitude was impressive.

Congratulations on your retirement! Your place in Costa Rica sounds wonderful. I'd love to see it sometime and try some of your produce. Do you grow my favorite fruit, cherimoya?

Business is good here. We get busloads of tourists this time of year, and they aren't shy with their money. Still, I wonder if there's more to life than knitting and weaving.

I'm glad you were able to gather lots of evidence from the tunnel. Finding it was therapeutic; giving me closure to a bad chapter in my life, and providing me an ounce of redemption for those poor girls who were killed at Bob's Beets. I pray each day for the capture of George Miller, and have faith that the day will come.

Send me a picture of your favorite beach. That will have to do for now.

Take care,

Esperanza

3

Ozwald Cosberg has a crewcut, wears designer sunglasses, and chews gum incessantly. He has a toned athletic body that the women find irresistible, which is good for "The Oz" who's a perpetual womanizer. He's broken many hearts, but that's okay because he's The Oz and another woman will be in his life soon. The Oz is so full of himself that he had three t-shirts made with "The Oz" on the front and "The Coz" on the back. He wears them everywhere, and even sleeps in one of them.

The Oz earned all-league honors as a halfback for the University of Idaho football team, quite an accomplishment for a horrendous team that won only one game all year. He excelled in the classroom too, maintaining a perfect 4.0 grade point average as a criminal justice major.

A recent graduate, The Oz has applied for several law enforcement positions throughout the country. Prospective employers have flown him in for interviews, and he's received three job offers— in Idaho, New York, and Texas.

The Oz agonizes over which job offer to accept. Working in his home state of Idaho is attractive because he's The Oz after all and he'd be close to friends, family, and women who consider him the big fish. Working in the bustle of New York City would be a drastic change from his rural Idaho and an exciting new chapter in his life. Working in Texas would be awesome because "everything's bigger in Texas." Indeed, the Texas job offers the largest pay. But in the mind of The Oz, "everything's bigger in Texas" means a certain two parts of the female anatomy.

Ozwald Cosberg, aka The Oz or The Coz if you're standing behind him, accepted the job offer in Texas with the Darby Police Department. He starts at the police academy on Monday.

4

The Oz reports to the police academy in Lubbock, Texas. He stays in a dorm room that's only slightly better than the one he had in college, only because he has no roommate. His desk and closet space are small but sufficient. His twin bed is questionable, as he must sleep diagonally to avoid having his feet hang over the edge. The view of a 3-story brick administrative building through his dirty window outright sucks, but The Oz is here to learn and knows the accommodations are a necessary speed bump on his road to professional success.

Learning comes easily, and The Oz regularly scores well in a curriculum that includes report writing, constitutional law and civil rights, state laws and local ordinances, accident investigation, patrol, traffic control, firearms, self-defense, first-aid, and emergency response. He regularly scores well in the extracurricular activities too, picking up women in questionable bars on weekends.

The physical training is child's play compared to the double-day football practices The Oz endured at the University of Idaho. His biggest challenge is the obstacle course, which involves scaling a 6-foot-high wall, jumping over a 5-foot-wide ditch, dragging 150 pounds for 50 feet, and running a quarter mile. It's exhausting, but as with most activities, The Oz excels.

After six months of intense training at the academy and graduating at the top of his class, The Oz swaggers in to the Darby Police Department with a shiny silver badge on his new police blues. His commander, Chief Johnson, is there to greet him with a firm handshake.

5

Chief Johnson partners The Oz with Officer Pete Landry, a 5-year veteran of the Darby police force, and the pairing works out nicely both personally and professionally. They couldn't be more different, but become the best of friends, and their car patrols through the streets of Darby become an effective deterrent to crime.

Officer Landry is a liberal African-American with a beer-belly and an unkempt police shirt that the Chief is always nagging him to tuck. He hails from the projects in the south side of Chicago, squeaked by night school to receive his criminal justice degree, and has a wife and three kids. The Oz is, well, he's The Oz, a conservative white kid with abundant muscles that fit nicely into his neatly pressed police uniform. He's single, comes from a wealthy Boise family, and breezed through college.

The Oz and Officer Landry jokingly dub themselves The Divergent Zebras. One of their patrols typically goes something like this:

0800   The Oz waits for Officer Landry in the driver's seat of their Crown Victoria with the engine idling.

0807   Officer Landry simultaneously jogs to the Crown Vic, tucks in his shirt, and puts on his police hat.

0808   They roll to fight crime.

0809   Officer Landry adjusts the radio from a country station to a hip-hop station.

0820   They stop at a donut shop where Officer Landry gets a jelly-filled donut and a fully-loaded coffee.

0830   They stop at a juice shop where The Oz gets a kale-mango smoothie with a zinc antioxidant boost.

0840   They roll to fight crime.

1040   A pit stop.

1045   Officer Landry shows The Oz the latest pictures of his kids on his phone.

1048   The Oz adjusts the radio from a hip-hop station to a country station.

1049   They roll to fight crime.

1230   They stop at a burger joint where Officer Landry gets a double bacon cheeseburger, fries, and a chocolate shake.

1245   They stop for fast Mexican food where The Oz gets a water and a salad bowl with steak, brown rice, black beans, guacamole, salsa, and cheese.

1315   Officer Landry takes the driver's seat and adjusts the radio from a country station to a hip-hop station.

1316   They roll to fight crime.

1515   A pit stop.

1520   Office Landry shows The Oz more of the latest pictures of his kids on his phone.

1523   The Oz adjusts the radio from a hip-hop station to a country station.

1524   They roll to fight crime.

1658   They park the Crown Vic back at the police station and gather their food garbage.

1700 They depart the Crown Vic and head to the locker room.

The Oz patrols with Officer Landry for two years, and as usual he excels. He garners Meritorious Service and Distinguished Service Medals, and is on the fast-track to becoming a detective. When word of a vacant detective position at the Lonebud Police Department gets out, The Oz applies. Chief Orville Pritchard is impressed with the application, and schedules an interview.

The Oz nails the interview, and Chief Pritchard is happy to hammer out the terms of a job offer to him. The Oz's salary would almost double, his moving expenses to Lonebud would be reimbursed, his work as a detective would have greater challenges and responsibilities, and his health, retirement, and leave benefits would increase substantially. The Oz accepts.

Officer Landry and The Oz do a final patrol through the streets of Darby in the Crown Vic. To please his departing partner, Officer Landry lets The Oz listen to country music on the radio the whole time. The catchy lyrics and intriguing stories of the country music begin to grow on the officer, and by the time he parks the Crown Vic back at the police station he's singing at the top of his lungs with The Oz and Kenny Chesney, "Everything gets hotter when the sun goes down."

The partners say goodbye back in the locker room with a firm handshake and then a hug. They vow to stay in touch and to have a drink sometime. And with that, The Divergent Zebras go their own ways.

6

As Malcolm O'Reilly's replacement on the Lonebud police force, The Oz works on the Bob's Beets case. He shows a natural aptitude for detective work— documenting and analyzing information efficiently, developing innovative information-gathering strategies, and collaborating well with the FBI, the Interpol, and the public. Nonetheless, not much progress is made on the case. Not much at all, until that scorching summer day when Chief Pritchard flips out.

7

Marge hovers outside of Chief Pritchard's office. Soon a couple coworkers join her. They strain to listen through the Chief's closed door while feigning interest in the postings on the bulletin board on the adjacent hallway wall.

The Chief is delivering an absolute tongue-lashing. The f-bombs fly freely, and the sh-bombs, and any other profanity bombs you can imagine. He tosses papers, pounds a fist against his desk, and even bounces a handful of popcorn off the door. The verbal tirade ends with an emphatic, "Get out!"

Who's the recipient of this verbal tirade? Who gets out of Chief Pritchard's office with tail tucked firmly between his legs? None other than that gumshoe prodigy, The Oz.

The Oz is visibly shaken. His fingers tremble and his shoulders slump. He averts his eyes from Marge and the others and quickly heads down the hallway. The Oz isn't used to failure, and his failure is epic. The Chief has placed him on a week of administrative leave.

The reason for the verbal tirade and subsequent administrative leave— an exclusive story on the Bob's Beets case that Heavy Chest Betty delivered last night. She reported that a lady named Esperanza Perez from Valvino, Chile is a key figure in the case. An unnamed police source told her that Ms. Perez can identify the man in the tuna photo that was so widely circulated, and that Ms. Perez was herself held captive by the man in Chile.

The Oz is that unnamed police source, as the Chief learned. The Oz confessed that he and Heavy Chest Betty had a mutual agreement that was consummated in seclusion at the Cuddly John Motel. The Chief and all of Texas watched the Heavy Chest Betty exclusive. Even George Miller, who was roasting a hot dog at a Shreveport KOA campground, watched on his portable television.

8

George Miller looks nothing like the man with the yellowfin tuna. Over 30 years have passed since the picture was taken, and that time has been hard on him. He's nearly bald, very gaunt, and his face has weathered worse than a sandstone formation in strong desert winds. The many wrinkles, pocks, and scars on his face are revolting. The long eyebrow, nose, and ear hairs are disgusting. The course stubble and mutton chops are hideous.

His right hip is cracked from the Bob's Beets blast and he walks stiffly, like the tin man in *The Wizard of Oz*, and like the tin man, George Miller doesn't have a heart. His metal cane helps immensely, allowing him to traverse uneven ground and long distances.

George now goes by the name Tucker Faulks, as shown on his fake ID card. Any dyslexic screw-up results in an awkward moment, which Tucker always savors.

Tucker has cleaned up a bit since roasting the hot dog at the Shreveport KOA campground two weeks ago. The unsightly facial hair is gone and he has new clothes. He shines up like a new penny for a cruise he's taking on a ship departing from the port of New Orleans, bound for Chile.

9

Chief Pritchard has cooled off after his tongue-lashing of The Oz. He reflects on the situation and realizes that he must notify Chilean police to watch out for George Miller, who now may know where to find his estranged daughter. And should George find Esperanza, she'll be safe with police protection, safe from a man very motivated to stifle her testimony against him.

The Chief also realizes that The Oz's information leak could be a blessing. The Bob's Beets case was going nowhere, but The Oz has inadvertently stirred the stagnant pot. He's dangled Esperanza as the carrot, and George is the rabbit.

Alright then, the Chief thinks after notifying Chilean police, *this could end quite well. Then again, it could end quite badly.* A devout Southern Baptist, the Chief says a prayer.

10

Despite his ailing hip, Tucker Faulks is having the time of his life on his cruise to Chile. His cruise ship, the Sea Glory, has a multi-story atrium with glass elevators, cabins with private balconies, a lavish dining room, and all the amenities. The 4,000 passengers enjoy a casino, library, fitness center, theater, miniature golf course, basketball court, rock climbing wall, and even a bowling alley and skydiving wind tunnel.

Tucker is happy to simply soak in a hot tub, read on a beach chair by the pool, catch an occasional show, over-indulge in food, and drink lots of alcohol. Lots of alcohol.

Today the Sea Glory makes the 10-hour, 48-mile trip through the Panama Canal from the Caribbean Sea to the Pacific Ocean. The process captivates Tucker. He spends all morning on the deck sipping margaritas and watching the three Gatun Locks fill and raise the Sea Glory 85 feet to Gatun Lake. He's fascinated by the electric locomotives on each side of the ship which have cables to keep the ship centered in the locks.

Tucker eats a buffet lunch while the Sea Glory crosses Gatun Lake, loading up on the meats and cheeses. Then it's on to his cabin for a much-needed siesta. After waking refreshed, Tucker returns to the deck to watch the Sea Glory step back down from Gatun Lake, passing through the Pedro Miguel Lock and the two Miraflores Locks to the Pacific Ocean.

It's dark now, and the bright lights of Panama City off the port side dazzle Tucker. The lights fade away as the Sea Glory journeys southward towards the coast of Columbia. With only darkness visible, Tucker heads for the Anchor Tavern for a pre-dinner aperitif.

He sips vermouth at the bar counter next to a portly middle-aged man with a beard but no mustache. The man drinks a frothy beer, which creates a foamy white mustache where he has none. It clashes horribly with his dyed black beard, but the man has an even more ridiculous-looking feature— a McDonald's golden arches tattoo on his chubby upper arm. "Where'd ya get the tattoo?" asks Tucker.

"N'awlins"

"I love N'awlins. What do you do there?"

"I don't do squat in N'awlins. We just like to party there. I'm a baker from Wichita. What do you do?"

"I'm a demolition contractor from Houston."

"Sounds like interesting work."

"It pays the bills."

"Bills, tell me about 'em. I think my wife is personally responsible for the surge in the American economy. Do you have a wife?"

Tucker's face turns somber. "I used to. I lost her and my son a long time ago. I have a daughter, but I haven't seen her in years. We don't seem to see eye to eye anymore."

"That's too bad. You should reach out to her."

"I am. She's in Chile. This is a reconciliation trip of sorts. I haven't held my daughter in years, but when I see her I'll be sure to hold her tight. Hold her tight and not let go."

"Good man. That's how it should be. You can't love your one and only daughter enough. Me, I've got four daughters. They're with my wife at some cheesy show in the theater. I couldn't stomach going to it, but I have no problem knocking down a few cold ones before dinner."

"Here here."

The two men take a drink. Just then, five ladies in evening gowns arrive. "Speak of the devils, here's my crew. Ladies, I'd like you to meet . . ."

"Tucker, pleased to meet you." They exchange smiles.

The portly man extends his hand. "I'm Jed. Pleased to meet you Tucker." They shake hands.

Jed's wife proclaims in a whiny nasal voice, "We have the eight o'clock seating dear."

"The dinner bell rings my friend," says Jed. He chugs his beer, replenishing the foamy white mustache. Jed gets up and his wife immediately dabs at the mustache with a tissue appearing from nowhere, like a rabbit out of a hat.

"Alright, have a good dinner," says Tucker. "Maybe see ya around the ship later."

"You bet. Best of luck with your daughter."

Tucker smiles and nods. Jed and crew depart. Tucker drains his vermouth and slams the glass on the bar counter. He mumbles to himself, "None needed."

11

Sergio and Isabel Delgado live with their six children in a 2-bedroom apartment in a lower middle-class neighborhood of Santiago. Their fingertips are split and calloused from working at a shoe factory six days a week. They earn meager wages, but with the two eldest children working and bringing in money, Sergio and Isabel plan to buy a home next year.

The two eldest are the identical twins Eduardo and Bernardo, each with dark straight hair, chiseled high cheekbones, and strong stocky physiques. The handsome 24-year-olds are policemen who patrol high crime areas of Santiago on foot.

After two years of deterring pickpockets, purse snatchers, car thieves, residential burglars, domestic terrorists, rowdy student demonstrators, and disruptive labor picketers, Eduardo and Bernardo have some exciting career news. They're home for dinner after a particularly trying shift.

Isabel has prepared palta reina, avocado stuffed with a prawn filling. "How was work today boys?" she asks.

In between bites an animated Bernardo says, "A guy was ransacking a home by the university. He had the homeowners tied up in the closet and was swinging a bat at us. Not a bad swing either, but we had to put him down, right Dado?"

An equally animated Eduardo says, "That's right, I lit him up with my taser, and then we freed the homeowners."

"Well done boys," says Sergio. The boys' siblings cheer.

"We might be done with this city crime sh . . . with this city crime stuff. We got an interesting offer from headquarters this morning, right Dado?"

"Yeah, they offered us a cushy temporary assignment up in the Andes, at a place called Valvino. They want us to protect some lady."

"She must be very important," says Sergio.

"We need you here," says Isabel.

"Can I come?" says Ernesto, the youngest sibling.

"Dado and I already discussed it. We need this. We need a break from the city, and we'll be back before you know it."

"I don't know," says Isabel, shaking her head anxiously.

"Our boys are men," says Sergio. "They have spoken."

"But honey, the people there might—"

"Enough. Respect their decision."

Head down, Isabel retreats to the kitchen. She returns with alfajores, big soft cookie sandwiches with a sweet caramel filling. "We have a special dessert," she says. "For a very special occasion, it turns out. Let's eat."

12

Dear Rudy,

You may not have heard that your replacement on the police force leaked out my location. As you know, I always have an eye on my back. And now I have more eyes on my back since your chief helped arrange for Chilean police to watch over me. I wish you were still on the police force to watch over me. Can I get your phone number? My number is 56-951-555-3902.

The policemen who protect me are young. I don't think I'm getting a top-notch team. They follow me everywhere, and one of them is even stationed outside my cabin at night. It's hard to lose so much privacy. My "Pearl of the Andes" has lost some of its luster.

Enough of my troubles, how are you? How's your crop of fruits and vegetables? Still going to the market once a week? Do you have a nice tan from lying on the beach and swimming in the ocean?

I think of your beaches often. I close my eyes and can almost smell the salt and hear the waves crashing. Last week I even dreamt about a beach. I woke up with my fingers in my hair. I think I was trying to brush the sand out. Isn't that crazy?

Sorry to bother you with my situation, but I feel better that you know. Don't worry about me, I'm sure I'm in good hands and will be fine. Keep in touch and I hope to see you again in the not-too-distant future.

Sincerely,

Esperanza

13

Doctor Snidely Fillmore mans the small infirmary on the stable bottom deck of the Sea Glory. A year removed from his residency at the Milan Clinic, Doctor Fillmore already grows tired of the nomadic life of a cruise ship doctor, and he's made the unpleasant discovery that he's susceptible to seasickness. The next port of call can't come soon enough in rough seas. A knock on the door interrupts the doctor, who's reading a medical journal. "Come in," he says.

Tucker enters with the aid of his cane. "Hi, are you the doctor?"

"Yes sir, I'm Doctor Fillmore. How can I help you, Mr. . . ."

"Mr. Faulks. My hip is bothering me."

"What happened?"

"Well, the hip's been bothering me for a while, and then I fell on Deck Three last night. I'm such a klutz."

"Let's take a look. If you could drop your pants please." Tucker drops his drawers and the doctor prods. It hurts like hell and Tucker groans. "I'd like to do an x-ray. It's three-hundred dollars. I can put it on your folio, and then you can get reimbursed by your insurance company later. Is that okay?"

"Three-hundred, huh? Tucker ponders. "What I really need is some pain medicine."

"I can prescribe that. What about the x-ray?"

"I'm gonna take a rain check on that. I'll go in for an x-ray when I get home if the hip still bothers me."

"Very well." Doctor Fillmore scribbles on a piece of paper. "Take this prescription to the pharmacist on Deck Eight, and try to stay off that leg."

"Will do, but if I have to walk somewhere my third leg will help." Tucker taps his cane.

"Alright then. Good luck to you Mr. Faulks."

"Thanks." They shake hands and Tucker hobbles out.

Once outside, he chuckles at the prescription in his hand, a prescription he plans on sharing.

14

Dear Esperanza,

I'm sorry to hear that you now need police protection. My replacement must be a fool. I'm sure everything will be alright, but if you ever need to reach me for anything, anything at all, my number is 506-294-555-3072.

I'm also sorry about you losing privacy. Has anyone discussed relocating you to a safer place? That would be a big lifestyle change, I know, but maybe one worth considering. Of course you're welcome to stay here anytime if you need to get away for a while.

The fruits and vegetables grow like weeds here, and I make about 10,000 colones a week at the market. That's my beer money, and the golden Imperial is superb.

I'm getting pretty tan from gardening, playing tennis, and walking the dog. I jump in the ocean to cool down, but I'm not one for sunbathing on the beach. My restless legs won't allow it.

Guess what? I'm learning Spanish! It's slow going for an old chap like me, but I hope to have a fluent conversation with you in Spanish someday. No ser divertido?

Keep me abreast of how things are going and don't hesitate to call if you need anything. I've got a beach umbrella waiting here for you when the time is right.

Sincerely,

Malcolm

15

Tucker rides in an opulent glass elevator to the pharmacy on Deck 8. He sees mostly blue outside; only a sliver of the Peruvian coast separates the calm Pacific Ocean from the sunny sky. A lone seagull keeps pace with the Sea Glory not 20 feet away. Tucker imagines being as free as the seagull, free from the potential consequences of his past reckless behavior, and free from the constant hip pain. The elevator bell dings at Deck 8 and Tucker is brought back to reality, the painful reality of hobbling to the pharmacy. A pharmacist is there to greet him. "Can I help you?"

"Yes, I have a prescription to fill." Tucker slides the prescription over.

"Can I see your ID please?" Tucker slides his ID over. "Thank you . . . Tucker Faulks. That will be fifty dollars Fucker, uhhh . . . Tucker."

The pharmacist cringes, but Tucker beams. "I think I should get the verbal abuse discount."

"I'm so sorry. That was bad. I can put the fifty on your folio, and then you can get—"

"Yeah, yeah, I know, get reimbursed by my insurance company. Here, here's the fifty." Tucker hands over two twenties and a ten.

"Thanks . . . Tucker. You're getting Percocet, pretty powerful stuff. Take one tablet every six hours as needed for the pain. Would you like further consultation?"

"No, I've heard quite enough, thank you."

"Right. Well then, please have a seat and we'll have your meds in just a few minutes."

16

Esperanza awakens to voices, the familiar voices of policemen Eduardo and Bernardo Delgado. Each morning at precisely eight the twins execute the changing of the guard, though not nearly as majestically as at Buckingham Palace.

This morning Bernardo replaces Eduardo, who was stationed outside of Esperanza's cabin all night. Other mornings Eduardo replaces Bernardo. They also trade off escorting Esperanza into Valvino, and catching up on sleep at the Hotel Abrego.

Esperanza rolls out of bed and gets ready for the day. Her primitive wood cabin is deceptive, as she has the conveniences of running water and electricity. After a breakfast of wheat toast and grape juice, she showers, brushes her teeth and hair, and throws on some clothes. The voices have stopped.

Esperanza emerges from the cabin in her flaming red and yellow wool poncho. Bernardo stands tall, armed with a Colt pistol and a taser. "Good morning Ednardo," she says. Because of their identical looks and irregular schedules, Esperanza never knows for sure if she's talking to Eduardo or Bernardo. So she simply calls both of them by the compound name "Ednardo."

"Good morning. How'd you sleep?"

"Terrific. I truly appreciate all that you and your brother do for me."

"No problem. Where to today?"

"I need to go see a friend."

Esperanza and Bernardo walk briskly on the dirt trail to Valvino on a spectacular sunny day. They come to a patch of the Sacred Flower of the Andes, a beautiful alpine shrub featuring arching branches with hairy green leaves and drooping clusters of magenta tubular flowers. Esperanza picks some of the flowers and makes a bouquet. Bernardo looks on inquisitively. "For my friend," she says.

"A boyfriend? I think he'd rather have a bouquet of cookies."

"I don't have a boyfriend."

"What, a pretty woman like you? Nonsense! I would be happy to be your boyfriend."

"Are you hitting on me?"

"No, of course not. Our relationship is strictly professional. But if I asked, would you go out with me?"

"I'm too old for you."

"Is that a 'no'?"

Esperanza sighs. "It's an ambiguous 'yes', but don't get any ideas. For future reference, are you Eduardo or Bernardo?"

"I'm Ednardo, remember?"

Esperanza smiles and shakes her head. She and Bernardo resume their brisk walk to Valvino. After half an hour they depart the dirt trail on the east side of town, and climb several andesitic stairs to the green lawn terrace of the Valvino cemetery.

The cemetery stares down at the beautiful verdant valleys, a heavenly setting and the ultimate final resting place. Esperanza finds the grave of Paola Ramos, the lady that took her under her wing when she first landed in Valvino. Bernardo backs off to give Esperanza some privacy, a commodity that she cherishes but doesn't get much anymore.

Esperanza lays the bouquet of Sacred Flowers of the Andes by Paola's granite headstone and removes three wilted bouquets. She kneels, bows her head, and murmurs:

Hello my friend. I miss you. I miss your nurturing hands and gentle ways. I think I've perfected that spiderling lace pattern you taught me. At least my customers seem to think so.

My deranged father I told you about, I think he's coming to find me, and if he does I'm afraid of what will happen. I don't know if I'm safe here anymore. I'm not sure if I should stay. If I leave, I don't know if I could still knit and weave for a living. That's the only skill I have, and for that I'm forever grateful to you. What should I do Paola?

My problem is trivial compared to the one you had. Cancer is so terrible. You were so courageous. I should have done more for you. I should have increased your morphine dose, regardless of what the doctor said. I'm so sorry.

Esperanza puts her hand to her mouth and then to Paola's headstone. She stands up and crosses herself. "Amen," she whispers. "Bye my friend."

17

Tucker limps down the gangway at the large seaport of Valparaiso, Chile. He creates a peculiar melody with his cane tapping the gangway like a metronome, and the wheels of his suitcase humming on the stippled metal surface. Soon the melody ends when he steps off the gangway onto terra firma.

The Percocet eases the pain of his hip but muddles his mind. Tucker takes one last look at the Sea Glory, which appears a bit jumbled, and then seeks the line for a taxi. After a 30-minute wait in line, Tucker gets in the back of a yellow and black taxi. The driver gets in after stowing Tucker's suitcase in the trunk. He turns to Tucker, who leans forward and says, "I'd like to go to the bus station."

The cabbie is Hans, the son of a Nazi war criminal who fled to Chile after World War II. Because of his father, the locals have harassed Hans his whole life, and he's a bitter man. Hans is incapable of being friendly with any of his customers, and affirms Tucker's destination request with a low grunt. Then he slams down the handle of an old taxi meter and drives away.

Hans navigates the streets of Valparaiso at a snail's pace. Tucker isn't quite sure if Hans is being overly cautious, extremely insecure, or is being greedy. He suspects the latter, and listens with disdain as the taxi meter ticks away like a time bomb, ready to explode when they reach the bus station. Tucker can't sit idly anymore. "Can ya speed it up a little buddy?" Hans responds with the low grunt.

They arrive at the bus station 45 minutes later, and indeed the taxi meter has exploded and inflicted serious damage to Tucker's wallet. Tucker pays the fare but leaves no tip, which elicits more than a grunt from Hans. "Here's your bag asshole," he says as he throws Tucker's suitcase to the ground.

Tucker counters with a solid, "Fuck you!" and strategically touches his metal cane against the side of the taxi as Hans drives away. Hans is unaware of Tucker's subtle touch, until he picks up his next customer and goes totally berserk at the sight of a 4-foot jagged scrape.

Tucker is satisfied with his revenge, and is rather jovial when he steps up to the ticket window at the bus station. "One-way ticket to Villa de Diego please." The attendant hands him the ticket and collects 20,000 pesos. After an annoying 2-hour wait, Tucker boards a rundown bus for the long ride to Villa de Diego, a small village only 20 miles from Valvino.

4

DADDY'S HERE

1

"That fucker!" shouts Tucker from his dumpy hotel room in Villa de Diego. His open suitcase reeks of whiskey, and shards of a bottle litter his clothes. Hans the cabbie has evened the score with his violent toss of Tucker's suitcase. A double whammy, Tucker doesn't have any more booze to chase down his Percocet and he doesn't have any more clean clothes to wear.

Tucker's room at the Garcia Inn has suffered from years of neglect. It sports a water-stained ceiling, a sloping food-stained floor, a sagging bed, and an unfinished bathroom with exposed pipes. But the worst feature is the abundance of large orb weaver spiders, which hang ominously outside his dirty window and inside his dark dank closet.

Nonetheless, this pitiful room is headquarters for his mission over the next few days, a mission which starts ungodly early with a short bus ride to Valvino. He boards a nearly empty bus at five-thirty in the morning, before the mass of tourists ride it to the popular Valvino market.

Tucker may be a drug-abusing murderer and rapist, but he's no dummy. He knows that people have daily rituals, even a pathetic person like himself. When he sold insurance he started the day with a jog, when he held Esperanza in the Andes tunnel he drank a cup of sweet tea in the evening, and when he held those seven girls in the Bob's Beets basement he worked on a crossword puzzle every afternoon.

Tucker steps off the bus with this knowledge. He has a hunch that whatever police are in Valvino for Esperanza, and undoubtedly they're here after Heavy Chest Betty disclosed her whereabouts, the police will start the day with a donut and coffee.

He finds the cobblestones of Valvino a nuisance to traverse with a bad hip and a cane, but perseveres looking and smelling for a bakery. A sweet yeast dough aroma flares his nostrils, and soon Tucker sits at a table in the corner of the one bakery in town.

Tucker observes the patrons while pretending to read the *Holy Bible* that he brought from his dumpy room at the Garcia Inn. He eats a wonderful blueberry lemon scone and drinks Dark Brazilian Santos coffee, which he poured himself from the generous selection of coffees on a counter by the cash register.

The bakery is crowded but quiet, as the locals focus on eating their baked goods. Tucker blends in well with the crowd, wearing a traditional wide-brim straw hat and a colorful wool poncho that he purchased in Villa de Diego. A cowbell on the door rings as customers trickle in and out. Tucker nearly chokes on his scone when the cowbell rings and Eduardo enters in his police khakis.

Eduardo, a handsome and charming young man in uniform, easily draws laughs from Carmen, the female proprietor twice his age, when he orders and chitchats. She's easy to talk to, and Eduardo divulges a couple things about himself.

"How long will you be in town?" asks Carmen.

"I'm not sure. Just long enough for a perceived threat to blow over."

"What's the threat?"

"I really can't say too much about the case, other than we're watching a lady very closely."

"A lucky gal, I'd be happy to be watched by you." Carmen blushes and shakes her head. "I can't believe I said that."

Eduardo's not sure how to respond and emits a nervous giggle. Tucker has heard all he needs to know, and can do without learning the ultimate outcome of Carmen's flirtation. He gets back to enjoying his scone and coffee, until Eduardo heads for the generous selection of coffees on the counter.

Tucker watches Eduardo, being careful not to be caught watching. He buries his face in the *Holy Bible*, periodically glancing over the top of the Good Book. Eduardo pours himself a cup of coffee from a pot on the counter, and sits down with the coffee and a chocolate donut only two tables away.

Eduardo sips his coffee and inhales his donut. He reads his phone and responds with texts, fortunate to have cell coverage. When the coffee is gone, he pours another cup from the same pot. He drinks this cup faster, and glances at his watch frequently. The clock on the wall reads seven-oh-five when Eduardo leaves.

Tucker leaves a few minutes later, having seen enough to formulate a plan. He thinks it will work, and is excited that after 15 years he can finally confront Andrea tomorrow, or Esperanza as she is now known.

2

Tucker sits at the same corner table in the Valvino bakery, wearing the traditional wide-brim straw hat and colorful wool poncho. Today he eats a wonderful cherry almond scone and drinks Colombian Supremo coffee. He's counting on the same policeman as yesterday coming in for a donut and coffee. Why wouldn't he, people have daily rituals. Tucker pretends to read the *Holy Bible,* and listens for the cowbell on the door.

The cowbell rings. A mother and her daughter, wearing a plaid school uniform, enter the bakery. They browse the impressive selection of baked goods. Tucker goes back to the *Holy Bible.*

The cowbell rings. A delivery man carries a 50-pound bag of coffee beans into the bakery, and Carmen escorts him to the kitchen. Tucker glances at the clock on the wall and starts to wonder if the policeman is coming. *Maybe he has a family emergency or overslept, maybe he has another assignment or is on vacation, maybe . . .*

The cowbell rings. It's him. Adrenaline courses through Tucker and his heart beats fast. He feels like a boxer answering the bell for round one, in the fight of his life.

Like yesterday, Eduardo charms Carmen with his order and chitchat. Then he pours himself a cup of coffee from a pot on the counter and sits down at a table across the room with the coffee and a chocolate donut. Tucker strains to watch Eduardo drink the coffee from a distance, while pretending to read the *Holy Bible.*

Eduardo blows on the hot coffee and sips it lightly. His sips get larger as the coffee cools, and when he tips back the coffee cup, Tucker's internal alarm goes off and he springs to action.

Tucker goes to Eduardo's pot of coffee and refills his own cup, but he also dumps a 10-day supply of crushed Percocet pills into the pot and swirls it. Tucker returns to his table and scans the room. No eyes are on him.

Eduardo tips back his coffee cup further now. A refill is imminent. Tucker's heart palpitates when the schoolgirls' mother approaches Eduardo's pot for a refill. He buries his face in the *Holy Bible* and, to calm himself, Tucker tries reading scripture for the first time in his life:

Fear not, for I am with you; be not dismayed, for I am your God; I will strengthen you, I will help you, I will uphold you with my righteous right hand.

The mother is smelling Eduardo's pot and an adjacent pot when Eduardo arrives for a refill. Eduardo pours the refill, as Tucker had hoped. "Best damn coffee I ever tasted," he says.

"And it gives me the jolt I need to get going. Can I pour you one?"

"I better not," says the mother. "I should stick to decaf," and she pours herself a cup from the adjacent pot.

"Okay ma'am, have a nice day." Eduardo returns to his table.

Tucker sighs and pats the *Holy Bible*. Then he strains over the top of the Sacred Writings, for which he has a new appreciation, to watch Eduardo drink the spiked coffee. The clock on the wall reads seven, and by seven-oh-five the spiked coffee is gone and Eduardo is out the door. People have daily rituals, and Eduardo doesn't violate the maxim.

The cowbell rings a final time as Tucker leaves the bakery and follows Eduardo from a comfortable distance. Tucker cracks a smile.

3

Eduardo blazes along the dirt trail to Esperanza's cabin to relieve Bernardo at precisely eight. With his bad hip, Tucker has a hard time keeping up, but maintains sight of Eduardo in the distance. That distance gradually shrinks as Eduardo periodically stops, bends over, and puts his hands on his knees.

Eduardo wobbles and shakes his head now. Tucker closes within 100 feet, knowing it won't be long. Eduardo stumbles another 10 steps and crumples onto the dirt headfirst, sending a small brown cloud into the air.

Tucker hurries to Eduardo and quickly takes his Colt pistol and taser and smashes his phone. He conceals the Colt and taser in pockets beneath his poncho, where his own Smith & Wesson pistol already resides. Tucker senses the policeman has brought him close to Esperanza, so he leaves the dirt trail and begins a stealthier walk through andesitic rock outcroppings.

He chooses his steps carefully, and after 10 minutes on his uneven route he stops to pop a couple Percocet pills for the pain. Tucker sees a lone cabin after another 10 minutes, with a policeman stationed outside. The policeman paces nervously and glances at his watch frequently. Tucker's own watch reads eight-fifteen. He hunkers down behind a large boulder and watches.

4

Esperanza brushes her wet black hair, which glistens like obsidian after her morning shower. She wonders, *Where are the voices? The voices are comforting and indicate a police presence.* Just then Bernardo speaks, "Esperanza? Are you awake?"

That's better. "Coming," she says. Esperanza opens the front door in her robe. "Good morning Ednardo."

"Good morning. My brother's running late. Probably overslept. I tried calling him but can't get through. Damn cell coverage. Why don't you have breakfast and finish getting dressed while I find him. It won't be long, thirty minutes tops."

Esperanza hasn't been alone in a month. "Are you sure it's okay?"

"You'll be fine, thirty minutes tops. Just lock the door, and you can always try calling me."

"Alright then, you better get going. See you soon." Feeling somewhat reassured, Esperanza closes and locks the door.

From his post behind the large boulder, Tucker watches Bernardo jog down the dirt trail. He knows time is of the essence, and he hobbles to the cabin as fast as he can. But fast is not careful and Tucker stumbles, saved only by a fortunate planting of his metal third leg.

He draws his Smith & Wesson and twists the locked knob of Esperanza's front door. Tucker rattles the locked doorknob in frustration, but easily finds another way in by breaking the adjacent window with his gun and reaching inside to unlock the doorknob.

Tucker systematically searches the cabin. He jabs at the pile of alpaca wool in the front room. He spots an orange juice carton on the kitchen counter next to a half-full glass of juice. He touches the carton and it's still cold. "Oh Noodle, thirsty?"

Tucker moves on to the bathroom, which still has condensation on the mirror after Esperanza's hot shower. He writes "daddy" on the mirror. "Oh Noodle, daddy's here."

In the bedroom the bed is unmade, three dresser drawers are open, and a robe is on the floor. Tucker has caught Esperanza off guard, and the only unsearched place in her cabin is in the bedroom closet. He points his Smith & Wesson at the closet door and jerks it open.

5

Bernardo jogs down the dirt trail. In the distance he sees a heap on the ground, which a condor investigates. He jogs faster, and soon he can discern that the heap wears a police uniform. Bernardo sprints to his brother and flips him on his back, and the condor decides to depart for another meal.

"Dado, hey Dado!" A panicked Bernardo slaps Eduardo, but he's unresponsive and vomit drips from his mouth and pools on the ground. "Oh shit!" Bernardo clears and wipes Eduardo's mouth with two fingers. Then he hears a shallow breath and finds a weak pulse on Eduardo's carotid. "Thank God," he says.

Bernardo drags Eduardo into the shade of a boulder and calls Doctor Ruiz, who he saw just last week for a wart removal. "Doctor, this is Bernardo Delgado."

"Oh yes, hello."

"Please help, my brother's unconscious. We're on the dirt trail out of town, near Esperanza Perez's place."

"I know where that is. What's going on? Is it a head wound?"

"I don't think so. He's barely breathing and he has a weak pulse. I found some vomit on his . . . Oh shit! I gotta go."

"What is it?"

"His gun and taser are gone. My God, Esperanza!"

"Esperanza?"

"Please hurry doc." Bernardo hangs up and immediately calls Esperanza.

6

Esperanza hides behind her wood cabin in tall brush, having heard the front window break while pouring orange juice in the kitchen. Trembling, she slowly pulls out her phone from her pants pocket to make a quiet and desperate plea to Bernardo for help. And that's when her phone blares a most ironic ringtone by the *Scorpions— Here I am. Rock you like a hurricane. Here I am. Rock you like a hurricane.*

Tucker hears the ringtone and lowers his Smith & Wesson that points at an empty closet. He runs, as best he can, out the back door of the cabin towards the music. Esperanza frantically answers her phone to stifle the *Scorpions* and to quietly speak with Bernardo. "Ednardo help! He's here. What should I—"

Gunfire echoes through the Andes, and three bullets whiz over Esperanza's head. The third bullet strikes a boulder and ricochets with a high-pitched whine, like in a gunfight scene in a classic western movie. Esperanza knows what to do, she runs like hell.

Bernardo hears the bullets, first through the phone and then through the rarefied air. His stomach churns. "Esperanza! Can you hear me?" Bernardo gets no response, only the grunting of a desperate woman and the thrashing of footsteps. He races back to the cabin.

Esperanza easily outruns the gimpy Tucker, but she's ill-equipped for a protracted chase, having fled her cabin hastily. She has no food or water, and wears only leather sandals, blue jeans, and a bright red t-shirt. Nights in the Andes are bitterly cold without wearing a heavy jacket or a wool poncho and a wool hat. Esperanza knows she must get back to Ednardo, either one of them.

She stops to catch her breath after putting some distance on Tucker, and whispers into her phone which still has Bernardo on the line. "Ednardo are you there?"

Bernardo speaks between gulps of air. "Esperanza, you're alright!"

"I'm scared. I don't see him, but I know he's out there. I'm in a small ravine. It goes by my cabin. You can follow it up to me. Please hurry, and be careful."

"On my way."

Bernardo snakes up the small ravine and quickly tires. The ravine is dry, but he struggles climbing the steep dirt and rock channel with patches of thick brush. His struggle becomes much worse when an unbearable pain jolts his knee and scrambles his mind.

Bernardo goes down and instinctively grabs his knee. It's wet, which puzzles him in a dry ravine. A thunder-like sound reverberates, which is equally puzzling on a clear day. And the red on his khaki pants makes no sense whatsoever.

Bernardo begins to regain his faculties, and when he sees the barrel of a gun in his face and a man standing over him, the situation becomes crystal clear. Bernardo slowly reaches for his Colt.

"Don't even think about it," says Tucker, "or the next bullet goes in your head." Bernardo gets the message and retracts his hand, even though he doesn't speak English.

Tucker examines Bernardo. "You look like that other cop who nosedived on the trail. Do you have a brother? Is he a cop?" Bernardo stares vacantly at Tucker. "You don't understand a word I'm saying, do you?" The blank stare persists.

Tucker tries again in Spanish and Bernardo lights up. "What did you do to my brother? You're going to pay for—"

"That's enough." Tucker presses the gun barrel against Bernardo's temple. "Are there any more cops around here?"

"Yes."

"How many more?"

"Fifty." Bernardo lies, an attempt at intimidation.

"Really. Fifty more you say. So that's fifty-two counting you and your brother. That's a full deck. I don't believe you, I don't think you're playing with a full deck." Tucker taps the gun barrel on Bernardo's cheek bone. "How many more?"

Bernardo stares impassively. "Right. Well then, I think we're finished here."

Tucker carefully extracts Bernardo's Colt and taser, maintaining his own gun against the prone policeman's temple. He stashes Bernardo's Colt in the pockets beneath his poncho, where Eduardo's weapons already reside. "I'm gonna let you live. I want you to mourn your brother's death." Bernardo doesn't correct him. "He sure could pack away those chocolate donuts."

Tucker raises Bernardo's taser and lowers his Smith & Wesson. Bernardo instinctively shields his face with his hands. "Buenas Noches mi amigo," says Tucker. He squeezes the trigger and two electrode darts strike Bernardo's chest, convulsing him into a world of black. Tucker tosses the spent taser aside, smashes Bernardo's phone, and resumes his search for Esperanza. "Ollie ollie oxen free. Do you hear me Noodle? Ollie ollie oxen free."

7

Eduardo sleeps on his back in a sterile hospital bed with his mouth open. An IV bag hangs on a metal pole above him, and slowly drains fluid through plastic tubing into a vein on the back of his hand. A heart monitor registers a strong and steady beat. A clean white curtain is gathered next to a large picture window, which frames a flagpole flying a limp Chilean flag.

Eduardo starts to wake up. His heavy eyelids strain to rise, and when they do his eyes strain to focus. He sees what appears to be a cutout of Jesus hanging from the ceiling. Eduardo pans to the right and sees a toilet with the lid up, and then pans back to the left. "What the hell?" he says. "Bernardo?"

"Dado, you're awake." Bernardo has his own IV bag and heart monitor, and a huge bandage wrapped on his right knee. "Welcome back."

"Back, from where? What the hell happened to me, and what the hell happened to you?"

"I talked to the doctor. You, my friend, nearly overdosed on pain killers."

"No way. I didn't take any—"

"But you did, you just didn't know it."

"The only thing I had today was a chocolate donut and . . . wait a minute, my last cup of coffee seemed a little bitter. Someone spiked it?"

"I think George Miller spiked it."

"George Miller, he's here?"

"The fucker shot me in the knee, and now he's going after Esperanza. We fucked up Dado."

An elderly nurse wearing a white hat with a red cross gives each Delgado brother a snack tray consisting of chicken bouillon, strawberry jello, and a cheese stick. She uncovers the bouillon and steam billows towards the Jesus cutout. "Enjoy," she says before darting out. The brothers stare at their trays and push them aside.

"The fucker tased me too," continues Bernardo. "I tried calling Esperanza after I got my wits back, but she didn't answer. Then I called headquarters. Chief Castro sent help for me and was going to organize a team to find Esperanza and take out Miller. She must be terrified running from him through the Andes."

"How did I get here?"

"I sent help for your sorry ass. You took a header on the way to Esperanza's cabin."

"Shit Bernardo, look at us. A couple of invalids. We did fuck up." Eduardo stuffs his cheese stick into his jello. "And we can't unfuck it."

8

Chief Pritchard sits back in his chair with his legs propped on his desk. He strokes his handlebar mustache with one hand, and holds the phone to his ear with the other. "Yes Chief Castro, I'll be in touch." He hangs up the phone, which rests on his lap, and makes another call. The Chief's tone becomes harsher. "Officer Cosberg, to my office."

The Oz knocks on the Chief's door within a minute. "Come on in . . . sit." The Chief drops his legs to the floor and leans forward. "You were a running back in college, right?"

"Yes sir."

"Well I'm handing you the ball."

"Sir?"

"I'm giving you a chance to right your wrong, on the Bob's Beets case."

"What can I do?"

"You can help Chilean police find Esperanza Perez. George Miller found her, and now she's running for her life."

The Oz bows his head. "Because of me he found her."

"It's not all your fault. Two Chilean policemen screwed up. They failed to capture George Miller, and now they're in the hospital stewing in their own juices." The Chief massages his knees, a treatment he does every few hours since taking bullets to both legs while delivering Popcorn Justice years ago. "I just got off the phone with Chief Castro in Chile. He's assembled an eight-man task force. They may not be as elite as the Navy Seals or the Army Rangers, but they're our best shot at safely retrieving Esperanza and capturing that Miller freak. They call themselves El Pulpo, and I want you to join them."

"Of course."

"Good. Marge will help you with the logistics of getting there. Any questions?"

"Just one. What's El Pulpo?"

"Hell if I know. You can ask a fellow Pulpo . . . Pulpoer . . . Pulposter. Shit, just look online."

9

Esperanza hears the gunshot that takes down Bernardo. She hopes the bullet has lodged in her evil father, preferably in the head or heart. She anxiously waits for Bernardo to join her and deliver the good news, but her hope ends abruptly with a shudder when she hears those hair-raising words, "Ollie ollie oxen free. Do you hear me Noodle? Ollie ollie oxen free."

"Ollie ollie oxen free," innocent words that innocent children shout in games like Kick the Can and Capture the Flag. The irony is lost on Esperanza, however, who never played those games during her nightmarish upbringing. All she knows is that her crazed father is near and she must run like hell again.

Esperanza runs up the small ravine. It steepens as she approaches the channel origin at a rocky mountain ridge. Her running slows to an exhausted scramble up the dirt and rock channel. She catches her breath at the ridge and peers down at the verdant valleys below her peaceful village, now rocked by violence. They are diverse and beautiful valleys, with thick evergreen forests, terraced vineyards, saturated meadows, bursting wildflowers, and serpentine dirt roads that provide access to the beauty.

Esperanza spots some familiar landmarks in her pearl town— the central plaza, the cemetery, and the patchy soccer field speckled with scurrying ant-like creatures. She finds her cabin and tries to estimate how far she's gone, but an ominous white flash interrupts her, the flash of sunlight on shiny metal. Her father's gun she surmises, so she hurriedly crosses over the ridge into a new watershed with a new set of challenges.

10

Tucker is better-equipped than Esperanza for a protracted chase, wearing that wide-brim straw hat and that wool poncho to warm himself through the cold Andes nights. He wears sturdy leather boots, which are invaluable in his search over irregular terrain, although the right boot takes little weight beneath his fragile hip. And he has that arsenal of weapons, thanks mostly to the Delgado brothers, to combat any resistance to his search. But like Esperanza, he has no food or water, and until he catches and kills Esperanza, he has no satisfactory outcome.

Tucker trudges on despite his bad wheel, scanning the mountainside for a daughter who can put him away. For- ever. His cane and the Percocet are his friends, enabling him to maintain a slow and steady pace through the Andes. He is the tortoise and Esperanza is the hare in a race that can have only one winner.

Spotting Esperanza in her bright red t-shirt on the barren mountainside is easy. When the red disappears behind a rocky mountain ridge, the tortoise knows exactly where to go, and 30 minutes later the tortoise is there.

11

Esperanza feels like she's in an entirely different world on the other side of the rocky ridge. She's on the leeward side, which is a desert and almost totally void of green in the distant valleys below, a stark contrast to the lush valleys on the Valvino side. The leeward valleys receive just a smattering of rainfall after the orographic effect wrings out most of the rainfall on the Valvino side. Without the rainfall agricultural is nonexistent, and the leeward valleys are sparsely populated and void of dirt roads which could take Esperanza to safety.

She traverses a small ravine like before, which is the closest topographic feature to a road. The dry ravine gets wider as dendritic tributaries join in, and after an hour of snaking down the steep dirt and rock channel Esperanza stops behind some thick brush and pulls out her phone. The breeze kicks up and feels good on the back of her sweaty neck.

Esperanza snaps a picture of the ravine looking downstream, which is where she's headed next. She checks her phone battery, which is at 90 percent since she charged it last night. She texts Bernardo, not wanting to project her voice, and attaches the picture.

Ednardo are you okay? Heading down this ravine. Psycho's behind me somewhere. Please help!

She immediately gets a response; *Can't send message, try again.*

"Damn," she says.

She repeats the futile exercise with Eduardo, the other Ednardo; *Can't send message, try again.* And finally with Malcolm, her friend and a detective she respects; *Can't send message, try again.* Esperanza puts the phone back in her pants pocket and looks skyward. *Please let me find cell coverage and let the messages go through. Please let them find me.*

The wind is stronger now and dark clouds move in. A large raindrop falls. Then some more. And then the heavens open up; such is the changeable weather in the Andes. The rain pummels Esperanza who's on the move again. She looks longingly at the dry desert valleys so far below.

Her blue jeans and bright red t-shirt darken and become heavy with rain. Her leather sandals are more like ice skates as she slips on the wet dirt and rocks in the ravine. Soon the ravine rages as the flashy tributaries deposit their loads. The cold whitewater nips at Esperanza's heels as she struggles up the steep muddy streambank.

She wills herself to the top of the streambank, shivering uncontrollably. Esperanza and her clothing are drenched, including her pants pocket where her phone resides. Her trembling hand nearly drops the phone as she pulls it out, and her heart skips a beat. The phone is her lifeline and she must keep it dry, but how?

Esperanza pats her body and sighs. She surveys the area for shelter and shakes her head. Her teeth start to chatter and, defeated, a tear drop rolls down her face to mingle with the rain drops on it. She reaches up with her left hand to wipe her face and . . . *yes, that will have to do!* Esperanza puts the phone under her dry left armpit and clamps down.

She gets moving again to stave off hypothermia, and discovers that the new phone placement slows her way down. She walks like a penguin with a broken wing, over slippery rocks and boulders, through patches of tall vegetation, above the raging ravine. She gradually descends to escape the colder temperatures of the higher elevations, still shivering uncontrollably.

Mercifully the rain starts to let up and the flashy ravine starts to recede. Esperanza is exhausted and thirsty, although she swallows some water by tipping her mouth to the weeping sky. Her stomach rumbles with nothing in it, having abandoned drinking the orange juice that she poured when Tucker came crashing through her front door. Dark will preside soon and she seeks shelter.

Esperanza's head swivels like a radar antenna as she walks, looking for a warm place to hunker down for the night. Her broken penguin wing has healed as the rain has stopped and she now carries her phone in her quivering hand. Dusk settles in as she detects a promising spot. It's a large boulder with an indentation and small overhang, a cave of sorts.

She steps by the boulder and undresses, kicking off her muddied sandals first. Then she takes off her saturated t-shirt, wringing it out into her mouth before hanging it on some nearby brush to dry. Finally, she hangs her jeans and undergarments on the brush. Esperanza is naked and drier and remarkably a little warmer. She hurriedly snaps a picture of the cave and then huddles inside it.

The cave is only three feet deep and three feet high so she sits. Esperanza rubs her body vigorously and the shivering stops, which makes texting much easier. She attaches the cave picture and sends another text to Bernardo.

At this cave now. Trying to get warm. Will stay here the night. Please help!

She immediately receives; *Can't send message, try again.* Texts to Eduardo and Malcolm have the same fate; *Can't send message, try again.*

"Damn," says Esperanza, who carefully places the phone on the dirt floor. She leans against the cave, worrying about falling asleep and not waking up, becoming a victim of hypothermia. But Esperanza is exhausted and warmer, and she starts to doze off.

12

Tucker joins that different world on the leeward side of the rocky ridge and looks around. He thinks Esperanza would travel down the small ravine that originates just below him. He opts not to do the same with his tender hip, fearing he couldn't get in the ravine, let alone out of it. So Tucker limps steadily along with his cane by the top of the ravine. He navigates downstream in search of his Noodle, and he's not alone. Mountain viscachas, common Andean rodents which look remarkably like long-tailed rabbits, curiously follow him by leaping through the rocks.

When the rain comes, Tucker's wide-brim straw hat protects his head and face. It even doubles as a cup when he flips it over to catch rainwater for drinking. His wool poncho absorbs the rain but insulates him from the cold, and his leather boots keep his feet toasty.

Tucker marvels at the whitewater in the ravine, which is actually brown from suspended sediment. *It churns like a diluted chocolate shake in a blender,* he thinks. *Or a dust devil in Kansas. Or a long-haired brunette blow-drying her hair. Or a . . . His mind wanders, which is the effect of the Percocet. He likes it to wander away from the pain of his hip, so he pops another pill and washes it down with a sip of water from his straw hat.

Tucker trudges on, still conversing in his head. *The rain is easing, or am I just imagining it? No, the whitewater is dissipating too.* A break in the clouds reveals the sun is low and dark is encroaching. Tucker is tired and hunts for a clearing to make camp for the night with a real campfire. A campfire is possible since Tucker carries a butane lighter in his pants pocket, an old habit from his freebasing days.

He only needs to find some fuel. Scraps of paper in his wallet, mostly old shopping lists, make a good starter. Tucker looks for some dry grass or shrubs. After five minutes of combing the area, he finds a small patch of puya plants, which resemble large pineapples. The puya die when they bloom after a few decades, and some of these puya have tall flower blooms. He slowly drags back a dead puya without his cane, and violently shakes the rainwater off of it.

The puya is semi-dry and combustible, he hopes. Tucker breaks up the puya and sets some pieces on top of crumpled paper, the scraps from his wallet. He flicks on the butane lighter and ignites the paper. It burns and dense smoke rises from the puya. Tucker blows on the puya 'til he's light-headed, trying to get it to flare.

The puya still smolders, and Tucker is resigned to a cold night, when a sudden gust brings flame. Tucker lights up like the flame and shouts, "Yeah baby!" He rubs his hands together by the growing fire, and sets his wet wool poncho and straw hat on a nearby rock to dry.

The fire warms Tucker, and it can help him with another issue— hunger. A few viscachas overlook the campsite from the rocks, trying to comprehend the crackling, glowing fire. If he can just shoot one of them, he can roast it and savor the meat. Tucker pulls out his Smith & Wesson from beneath his poncho. He aims at the largest viscacha and pulls the trigger. Gunfire echoes through the Andes.

13

A busload of tourists slowly disembarks at the Valvino market. They are old and young, Latino and Caucasian, fit and obese. They push strollers and walkers, wear cameras and gaudy necklaces around their necks, and carry purses and selfie sticks. A young couple contorts for a picture by the bus, with selfie stick held high and lips pressed together.

Merchants put the final touches on their booths. Esperanza smooths out creases in her wool hats and ponchos. A gray-haired lady and a handsome young man approach. They browse through her collection of wool wall hangings and settle on a coarse one in a rainbow of colors. "How much for this one?" asks the gray-haired lady.

"For you, ten-thousand pesos."

"I'll give you twenty-thousand honey."

"But ma'am it's only ten-thousand."

"I want you to have twenty-thousand sweetheart."

Esperanza is dumbfounded by the lady's generosity and the terms of endearment. She looks closely at her and the handsome young man. Their faces are vaguely familiar, but she's not sure why. Then it hits her, and she nearly faints.

"Mom, Billy, is that you?"

"It's been so long dear."

"But I don't understand, how can you—"

"We can and we did." Esperanza's mom and Billy open their arms and Esperanza engulfs them. They laugh and cry and . . .

Esperanza awakens with a jump, startled by Tucker's loud gunshot at the large viscacha. Her heart pounds at the proximity of the blast. She urgently resends the texts to her prospective rescuers and again each time gets; *Can't send message, try again.* Desperate, she steps outside the cave into the darkness, naked and shivering again, and climbs onto a nearby boulder. She raises her phone skyward and resends the texts once more with shaking fingers.

Esperanza struggles to balance on the boulder, and thinks she must look like a pornographic Statue of Liberty, but she doesn't care, her life is at stake and this is her only salvation. Miraculously, the higher phone position provides better transmission and her messages are sent. "Yes!" she exclaims, and quickly climbs down from the boulder and retreats to her cave. She again warms her body by rubbing it vigorously. Her extremities get some color back and the shivering subsides.

Not wanting to miss a response, as unlikely as that would be in the cave, Esperanza stares vigilantly at her phone on the dirt floor.

5

RIDE OF THE VALKYRIES

1

Malcolm swats a backhand winner to take a rare match against Pablo, 6-4, 6-4. "Looks like I buy the beer today," says Pablo who extends his hand at the net of the red clay court. Malcolm shakes it.

"It's about time," says Malcolm. They towel off, pack their tennis bags, and deposit their clay-stained towels in a bin on the way to the bar at the tennis club. Inside the bar, a score of sweaty people sits beneath whirling fans, conversing and imbibing.

Pablo slaps a couple of bills on the bar. "Two Imperials please," he says. The bartender fills two frosty mugs, which Pablo delivers to the table where Malcolm sits.

Malcolm is transfixed on a televised cricket match. "The announcer said the bowler threw a beamer. What's a beamer?"

"Everyone knows a beamer's a German car. Are you saying the bowler threw a—"

"No, I'm not. Never mind." Malcolm raises his mug. "Well, down the hatch." Pablo raises his mug and they take healthy swigs, punctuated by emphatic quenched-thirst grunts. Two women at the next table shoot them a disgusted glance.

"I think they like us," says Pablo.

"What's not to like?" Malcolm's phone buzzes. "Hold on a sec." He reads a text and his face goes somber. "I gotta go." He gets up to leave.

"What is it Malcolm?"

"I gotta go."

2

"Damn vermin!" Tucker is pissed that his shot at the large viscacha whizzed overhead into the night. The viscacha and his buddies scampered away, and Tucker is resigned to lying by his toasty fire with no plate of meat. His stomach aches, his hip throbs, and his cane hand is blistered, which can mean only one thing, time for another Percocet.

Tucker nearly gags dry-swallowing the pill. The bright fire contracts his pupils, and his surroundings appear almost pitch black. Soon they are pitch black after the Percocet kicks in and his eyes close. The blackness spins like a black hole and, just as light can't escape a black hole, Tucker can't escape sleep. He snores contentedly with an open mouth, and dreams wishfully of a juicy double bacon cheeseburger.

3

Malcolm buckles his seatbelt for landing on the Air Andes redeye flight from Santiago to Peralsco. A poor farming community, Peralsco has many struggling ranchers, dairy farmers, and vintners who promote their inexpensive wines. And it has the closest commercial airport to Valvino, where Malcolm can begin his search for Esperanza, whose desperate text at the tennis club rattled him like a quake. Malcolm felt overwhelming guilt after reassuring her days ago that Miller could not breach her police protection.

The earlier flight to Santiago on Air Andes was good, with little air turbulence and few interruptions to his contemplation of Sudoku puzzles. Malcolm's neighbor didn't talk excessively, didn't encroach into his seat, and most importantly didn't smell bad. At snack time the flight attendant gave him an entire can of soda to wash down three bags of peanuts. And when landing in Santiago the view was spectacular, modern skyscrapers lit up at the base of the Andes, including the 64-story Gran Torre Santiago, the tallest building in Latin America.

Successfully buckled in for landing in Peralsco, Malcolm grabs the barf bag from the seat back in front of him and stuffs it in his coat pocket. He likes the red Air Andes icon on the bag, with twin mountain peaks that become twin "A"s when the vapor trail from a jet crosses the peaks, and thinks it will make a good addition to his barf bag collection.

The dawn landing in Peralsco is nothing like the spectacular night landing in Santiago, a smattering of dimly lit ranch houses surrounded by dirt and resting livestock. The turboprops reverse thrust after touchdown, and the aircraft slows abruptly and exits the runway. Cruising on the taxiway to the gate, Malcolm reads Esperanza's desperate text one more time.

Rudy help! Sheltering for the night in this cave. The psycho's still after me. Heading downslope towards desert in morning. Wearing red shirt. Cold and thirsty.

And he rereads his reassuring response.

On my way. Talked to former chief. Says trained task force will be looking for you. I can track you. Accept text from mobile location company. Keep sending texts. How much battery left?

Satisfied at his response, Malcolm puts his phone away and fidgets with the armrest while waiting endlessly for the plane to park. A flight attendant announces, "Welcome to Peralsco, the local time is six-twenty a.m.," and then Malcolm lurches forward as the plane comes to an abrupt stop. The "Fasten Seatbelt" light goes out and Malcolm immediately stands and hunches over to strap on his backpack. "Excuse me, family emergency," he says to his neighbor as he squeezes by his legs and moves to the aisle. The neighbor shoots him the stink eye, but Malcolm is already down the aisle. He's the sixth one out after the cabin door opens, which in his mind is five too many.

4

Malcolm has busted his butt all night to get to Peralsco. By catching a flight just as it was leaving Costa Rica, having a short layover in Santiago, and riding a strong tailwind, Malcolm has minimized his travel time, but thinks he can do better. He hurries.

Without a suitcase to collect on the luggage carousel, Malcolm speeds directly to ground transportation, which is located on a crumbling street just outside a voluminous rusted metal hangar. Not a single bus, taxi, Uber, or shuttle goes by at this quiet hour, only some bleary-eyed drivers of passenger cars picking up their friends or loved ones.

Malcolm enters the hangar to check for a posted bus schedule and determines that the next bus to Valvino departs at seven a.m. Not confident in his translation of Spanish, he turns to a man in grease-stained blue overalls and asks, "Habla inglés?"

"Hell yeah. Cy Clark, damn glad to meet ya." Cy stares oddly at Malcolm and sticks out his greasy hand.

Malcolm reluctantly shakes it. "Hi, I'm Malcolm O'Reilly. Are you American?"

"You bet, as American as shitty war policy."

Malcolm is dumbfounded by the response. "So, I want to ask you about the bus to Valvino."

"Seven, ten, and thirteen."

"Excuse me?"

"It leaves at oh seven-hundred, ten-hundred, and thirteen-hundred hours. That's military time for—"

"Got it, thank you." Malcolm starts for the restroom at the back of the hanger to relieve himself and clean his greasy hand. He doesn't get far.

"You should know the oh seven-hundred won't get ya to Valvino 'til around eleven-hundred."

"But doesn't the schedule say—"

"Screw the schedule. The oh seven-hundred is notoriously late. Always breakin' down, or in line for petrol, or replacin' a driver who overslept. It's always somethin'."

"Eleven is too late. Is there any other way?"

"You could take a taxi or an Uber, but they'll charge you a fortune. I'll only charge you seventy-thousand pesos."

"To take your car?"

"No, to take my plane."

Malcolm is dumbfounded again. "You have a plane?"

"Workin' on it right now. Just took a little potty break."

Malcolm's greasy hand feels much dirtier. "I didn't think Valvino had an airport."

"It doesn't, don't need one. Just need a clear and level patch of ground and I'll set 'er down. Come with me."

They walk across the hangar to a row of crop dusters. Tools and oily rags litter the cracked concrete floor. Halogen spotlights on tripods supplement the inadequate fluorescent lighting from high above. Windows are open to vent the nasty industrial odors. They are alone.

Cy stops at a vintage yellow crop duster and smiles. "This one's mine. Ain't she sweet?"

Malcolm considers the chipped paint, the cracked windshield, and the torn vinyl seats and lies. "A real gem."

"Just need to finish changing the plugs and topping off the fuel and oil. Give me twenty minutes and we can be on our way. I need to get back before lunch to spray my grapes."

"You grow grapes?"

"I make wine, mostly Merlot but the Carmenère does well too. I'll bring some with us."

"That's not necessary."

"I insist." Cy grabs a pair of goggles from the open cockpit. "I insist you wear these too. I wouldn't want you to get a bug in your eye."

Malcolm takes the goggles. Butterflies fill his stomach and he wonders if this is a good idea. But he must find Esperanza, and time is of the essence. Cy grabs another pair of goggles from the cockpit and dangles them, revealing only a single lens. "These are mine. The lens fell out, but havin' a glass eye I figured I didn't need to replace it." The butterflies swarm through the rest of Malcolm's body.

"I didn't want to say anything, but I thought you might have a glass eye. How'd you lose it?"

"Nam. Fuckin' Vietnam. Took some shrapnel in the face. After that I got my Purple Heart and an Honorable Discharge and said adiós to the U.S. of A. Came here to live the good life on my veteran benefits."

"Thank you for your service. I'll be back in twenty minutes."

5

Esperanza grows tired staring at her phone in the dirt and falls asleep lightly. She imagines incoming texts in her groggy state and perks up, only to deflate each time after realizing the truth. Hours pass, and when the cold becomes unbearable even in the cave, Esperanza abandons the idea of sleeping and springs into action.

She puts on her hanging clothes, which are somewhat drier from the light breeze, and does a few jumping jacks to warm up. She climbs up to her broadcasting boulder and raises her phone skyward. Esperanza waits. And waits more, the light breeze striking her body like a medieval stoning.

And then music, the buzz of her phone. No, two buzzes. They create the best symphony of her troubled life. Esperanza quickly climbs down from the boulder and retreats to her cave, where she excitedly reads each text.

On my way. Talked to former chief. Says trained task force will be looking for you. I can track you. Accept text from mobile location company. Keep sending texts. How much battery left?

Welcome to ML4U mobile locate. To share phone's location, reply YES. To end sharing, reply STOP. For info or terms, reply HELP. Message & data rates apply.

She composes a response to Malcolm and the obvious "YES" response to ML4U, and climbs back up to her broadcasting boulder. "Thank you," she mouths when her messages transmit, but her thankfulness is short-lived and she lets out a scream of terror when her cold fingers fumble her phone and it falls far below onto the wet ground.

6

The hangar bathroom is filthy, and Malcolm contributes to the filth by pissing in a toilet that won't flush and by washing his hands and coating the porcelain sink with a greasy film. He feels no remorse, just a whole lot better about his empty bladder and his clean hands. Stepping out of the bathroom, his phone buzzes. A text from Esperanza.

Rudy, I shared my phone location. Can you tell where I am? Battery down to 55%. Watching for task force and for you. Can't sleep, heading to warmer desert. Will send more texts and pictures.

As a law enforcement retiree, Malcolm has full health coverage and a nice pension. But his best benefit, under the circumstances, is his free subscription to the ML4U mobile phone tracking service. As long as his phone and a target phone are on and have cell coverage, he can visit the ML4U website and see a map showing the location of the target phone.

Malcolm visits the website and gets Esperanza's last known phone location, surrounded by a circle with a 1/2-mile radius to reflect location accuracy. The circle lies on a satellite image of the west slope of the Andes, where Esperanza runs for her life. Armed with this image on his phone, Malcolm goes back to his one-eyed wino pilot to chart their course.

"Shit, not gonna land there," says Cy while studying Esperanza's location on the satellite image. "Unless it's a crash landing. Didn't you wanna go to Valvino?"

"Yes. I was just trying to get closer."

"Closer? Closer to what? What's in the circle, and what's in your backpack? Are you some kind of drug runner?"

"No!"

"A bounty hunter. You're a goddamn bounty hunter."

"No! Just looking for a friend."

"A friend? Oh, I get it, must be of the female variety. Gimme that phone." Cy scrolls through the satellite image until it shows Valvino. "Not gonna land there either, no clear patches." Cy scrolls some more and taps the image on the phone. "Here. Here's where we can land." He points to the flat desert below Esperanza's circle. "Gonna cost you though, a hundred-and-fifty-thousand pesos with the booking change."

"Are you sure you can land there?"

"Shit yeah. The baked sand is practically a runway. I could land a washing machine in that desert." Malcolm digs into his wallet and hands over the money. They shake hands to consummate the deal, and Malcolm gets a greasy hand again. He puts on his goggles, leaving a smudge on the band, fearful of what's to come.

7

As an artisan, Esperanza appreciates vibrant colors, rich textures, and intricate patterns in all art media. But she despises the intricate spider web pattern in the broken glass screen of her phone. It's as if a spider has emerged from the web to sink its sharp fangs deep into her flesh. The spider bite becomes unbearable when she discovers that her phone won't turn on.

She depresses the power button and gives the phone a violent paint-mixer shake. Her mind is in turmoil when it won't turn on after three attempts. *I must stay by my cave and wait for Malcolm. He can track me here. No, I must keep moving, keep the blood flowing, keep ahead of the psycho. But how will Malcolm find me?*

Esperanza decides to head downslope towards the desert as originally planned. She walks above the ravine, which glistens with trickling runoff under the light of a waning moon. When the moon ducks behind a mountain peak, darkness envelops her cold damp body, and each of her steps becomes an uncertain maneuver.

8

Cy checks the area by the propeller of his crop duster. "Clear," he yells before starting the engine, which sends a puff of black smoke into the hangar. Cy and Malcolm jiggle with the hum of the engine, and then Cy eases the throttle forward and rolls the plane ahead. Malcolm fidgets nervously with the strap on his backpack in the seat behind Cy. He's thankful he can't see Cy's face, with his odd one-eyed stare through the goggles with a missing lens. His own goggles are antiquated, and he thinks he must be quite a sight too.

They pause at the runway threshold while Cy scans for air traffic and gets clearance for takeoff. Malcolm clenches his teeth and, for the fourth time in his life, he feels near death. Suddenly they accelerate down the runway and takeoff flawlessly into a brightening sky. Malcolm unclenches his teeth and blows a thunderous sigh.

Safely at cruising altitude, Cy uncorks a bottle of his finest Merlot. He offers the first sip to Malcolm, straining backward with the bottle against a strong wind. Malcolm holds up his hand to refuse the bottle, being more of a beer connoisseur. Cy won't take "no" for an answer, and when he thrusts the bottle out again Malcolm reconsiders. *Do I really want this maniac drinking the whole damn bottle? I could probably use a few shots to settle my nerves.* Malcolm grabs the bottle.

The label is nice, featuring the very vintage yellow crop duster in which he rides. Malcolm tips back the bottle. It's a dry wine and tastes pretty good. He smiles at the thought of how his wife Helen, a real wine connoisseur, might have described it— *fruity with easy tannins and oak.* Or *smooth and structured with earthy flavors and a soft finish.* Or *rich, full-bodied, not too acidic, and pairs well with chicken and other light meats.*

Malcolm tips back the bottle a few more times, and when he passes it back to Cy it's half gone. Cy shakes the bottle and notes the emptiness, and gives Malcolm an approving thumbs-up sign. Cy drains the bottle in a prolonged chug and tosses it aside. Malcolm worries about the rush of alcohol now coursing through his pilot, and about where the bottle will land with deadly force.

His worries turn to his stomach, which is not processing the Merlot very well, especially after strong turbulence buffets the tiny crop duster as it crests the Andes. Malcolm digs in his backpack for that Air Andes barf bag, willing to sacrifice the new addition to his collection, but it's too late. He spews over the side into the forceful wind, and it disperses like an aerosol spray.

Cy is oblivious to the eruption, concentrating on holding the yoke tightly and keeping the aircraft level. "Is that all you got?" he shouts to the wind. Malcolm's purge has him feeling better, and when the turbulence subsides on the leeward side of the Andes he's totally revitalized.

The leeward side. Esperanza's down there. I must look for her, reflects Malcolm. He scans below for a red shirt, but the limited light and tricky shadows offer little hope of detection. *If only the sun was higher. An hour, maybe forty-five minutes more. I could spot her then.*

Malcolm watches Cy for signs of inebriation, not that Malcolm could do anything about flying the plane. Cy hums the triumphant *Ride of the Valkyries*, but otherwise shows no ill effects from the Merlot. He flies the plane smoothly, and Malcolm gains confidence in his pilot.

Malcolm continues to check for Esperanza below. When Cy emphatically points his finger down a few times, Malcolm does a double take. *Did the one-eyed son-of-a-bitch actually find her?* he wonders. Cy suddenly pushes the yoke forward. Malcolm's stomach drops instantly and is severely tested a second time. He thinks maybe the alcohol has got the best of Cy, but then realizes they are simply descending to land.

9

The desert. Esperanza knows it's out there, but she can't see it in the pre-dawn darkness. She longs for its nourishing warmth, but for now must endure damp and frigid clothes. Her pace has slowed since twisting and gashing an ankle on a protruding rock in the darkness of night. It swells with fluid and drips with blood. The desert. It can be hers today despite the slower pace. Medical treatment. It won't be hers for perhaps days.

Her phone is dead, and she will be too if she doesn't get some fresh water. Muddy water dribbles in the ravine. Acidic water resides in desert cacti. She's not about to drink her own urine. Not yet.

Esperanza plods along on fumes after sleeping only intermittently in the cave. She passes an old campfire with rusted tin cans lying in ash, and imagines the taste of sweet and tangy pork and beans. Her stomach growls. She sees a dead condor with a broken wing on the ground and pauses to say a prayer. She hears a distant single-engine propeller plane and waves her arms frantically, despite knowing she won't be seen in the dull light of the emerging day.

Daybreak finally arrives. Her spirits rise with the departure of darkness. A gentle breeze stirs up, sparrows and finches chirp, and the approaching desert comes into focus. Direct sunlight won't strike Esperanza for a while in the shadow of the Andes, but having descended thousands of feet, the air is already warmer. The gentle breeze intensifies, and soon it ripples her red t-shirt and tousles her long silky black hair. She welcomes the natural clothes dryer. With her head back and limbs spread into the wind, Esperanza savors the sirocco-like blast for a few minutes.

And then she plays a hunch; she holds up her dead phone into the wind. After a few minutes Esperanza brings it down and presses the power button. To her amazement, the intricate spider web pattern in the broken glass screen of her phone lights up. "Yes!" she says, realizing her phone wasn't ruined after all, it was just wet. She snaps a picture of the desert and attaches it to a new message.

Rudy, I see the desert. Attached is a picture. Can you locate me? Battery down to 35%. Getting warmer and drier. Hurt my ankle and need water. Will rest and wait here.

Esperanza sends the message and waits with fingers crossed; *Can't send message, try again.* "Damn," she says. The spider bites again.

10

Cy and Malcolm descend in the vintage yellow crop duster to the baked sand of the desert. Cy turns the plane into the strong breeze for maximum lift, and touches it down in the early morning light. The wheels send a puff of sand into the breeze, which whisks away the tiny beige grains. The plane coasts to a quick stop and Cy cuts the engine.

Malcolm's goggles are off before the last revolution of the propeller. He rubs his eyes and stretches his arms. Cy removes his single-lensed goggles, flips some switches on the instrument panel, and turns to Malcolm. "Hell of a ride, eh?"

"Or a ride from hell."

"What, an unsatisfied customer?"

"It wasn't you; it was the damn turbulence. Had to deposit your fine wine over the side."

"Welcome to the Andean gut buster club. Happens to us all at some point." Cy disembarks onto the wing with some reading material. "What's the plan now boss, you go find your girlfriend?"

Malcolm joins Cy on the wing. "My friend . . . I go find my friend." Malcolm pulls out his phone and contemplates their current location courtesy of GPS, and the 1/2-mile-radius circle, Esperanza's last known location. "Think I'll head northeast into the foothills."

"When will you be back?"

"By dark."

"And if you're not?"

"Then you leave."

"We're gonna have to get creative to fit your girlfriend . . . uh . . . your friend onboard. You and your friend will have to get cozy, but I'm sure you're okay with that."

"I have to find her first. What'll you do while I'm gone?"

"Me? I've got some reading material, Playboy magazines. Did you know they stopped puttin' naked women in there, and now they're puttin' 'em in naked again? Can't make up their minds I guess. I say keep some clothes on 'em and leave something to the imagination."

"Alright then, I'll be off." Malcolm gathers his backpack and drinks from the water bottle in the side pocket. He steps down from the plane and peers back at Cy, who's rotated his magazine to view the centerfold. Cy tilts his head and stares oddly at Miss September, as only Cy can.

11

Chief Pritchard was right when he said the eight-man task force El Pulpo may not be as elite as the Navy Seals or the Army Rangers. What he failed to know was that El Pulpo may not be as elite as even the Keystone Kops. Without a significant budget, El Pulpo doesn't have the resources to be an effective search and rescue unit. Four of the men of El Pulpo, which the inquisitive Oz learned translates to "The Octopus," are not men at all, but are mules who transport the four actual men.

The mules are old and underfed, and their endurance and packing capacity are diminished. They are obedient but move slowly, which does not bode well for Esperanza. And who are the actual men of El Pulpo who ride on the mules? None other than recuperating policemen Eduardo and Bernardo Delgado, and Luta Malala and his son Leti.

Luta has neatly-combed short black hair, whereas Leti has frizzy long bleached blonde hair that screams I am my own person, nothing like my old man. Once a promising guitarist in Hawaii, Luta switched to the four-string ukulele when his left hand switched to four digits after a chainsaw accident. Soon thereafter his cheating wife left him for another musician.

So Luta and Leti left Hawaii with the last of their money on a cargo ship bound for South America. After a year crisscrossing the continent doing odd jobs, they ran out of money and energy and became homeless. They often don't know from where their next meal will come, and sport thin frames, contrary to many of their Samoan brethren. Sometimes a meal's from a food closet, but when the closet door shuts it's from a pungent dumpster, or a passerby who heeds their pathetic sign, "Spread some cheese on these broke crackers."

They survive day-to-day, mostly on handouts but partially on Luta's ukulele skills, which bring in some coinage. That all changed the day they came to Valvino and met Chief Castro.

The meeting was not under ideal circumstances, as Luta and Leti were brought in for shoplifting. Seems a couple of Moon Pies had their names on them. But the Chief took an immediate liking to the Samoans, who smiled politely and responded honestly throughout their interrogation. He empathized with their plight of being homeless, and offered them part-time work cleaning the bathrooms at the police station in exchange for some hot meals, which they happily accepted.

Luta and Leti watched the policemen at the gun range during breaks from bathroom detail. Often they pointed their filthy mops at various targets, mimicking the shooting of rifles. Chief Castro, seeing this faux firing one day, arranged to have them shoot for real as a Christmas bonus. They proved to be quite adept with a trigger, producing bullet spray patterns not so different from the policemen.

Chief Castro took notice of their shooting talents, and let them tag along on traffic stops, domestic violence calls, and even on drug raids. When El Pulpo was assembled, the Chief didn't hesitate selecting them for duty, especially since the price was right, some more hot meals. And now they answer the call, poised on their mules toting Remington pistols, eager to help.

Eduardo and Bernardo desperately pleaded with Chief Castro to let them join El Pulpo. A disgrace to themselves and their family, Eduardo played the purgatory card, "I know we'll go to hell Chief, unless we can make things right."

"We must save Esperanza, and in doing so we save ourselves," added Bernardo. With tears welling up in their eyes and rosary beads fumbling nervously in their hands, the Chief had no choice. The Delgado brothers were discharged from the hospital this morning.

And now here they sit on their mules, Bernardo with his knee heavily bandaged and Eduardo with only some paleness after his near fatal overdose. They sport Winchester rifles and know how to use them.

Chief Castro agreed to expand El Pulpo to 10 after conversing with American Police Chief Orville Pritchard, who explained his stake in finding Esperanza and Miller. So El Pulpo added a young hot-shot American cop and a trusty old mule, The Oz and Sylbuster.

The Oz squirms trying to get comfortable on Sylbuster. Having never ridden a mule or any other animal for that matter, The Oz has big eyes and grips the reins tightly. He appears nervous and insecure, nothing like the confident football star and policeman who excels at most activities. And he's exhausted after flying all night to be here. The Beretta pistol holstered on his hip jostles as Sylbuster, the rear mule in the mule train, steps forward. El Pulpo, an eclectic group of man and mule, sets out to find a desperate Esperanza and a ruthless Miller.

12

Tucker's juicy double bacon cheeseburger dream had him salivating briefly, but after a night of open-mouth sleeping his mouth is dry. Daylight wakes him by the dying fire and he smells burnt rubber. He examines the rubber sole of his right boot and sees that it's morphed into what appears to be the Madonna. "Shit, no way!" exclaims Tucker in amazement.

He takes a few test steps on the Catholic icon, getting a minute pleasure from it, until he stumbles. Tucker grabs his cane and tries again without stumbling, but his distorted rubber sole definitely complicates walking on his bad right hip, which he must do to find and kill Esperanza.

Tucker puts on his wool poncho and straw hat, which dried nicely on the rock by the fire. His stomach aches even more from hunger, so he welcomes the return of the curious viscachas. He slowly limps along after them with cane in one hand and gun in the other. The rabbit-like rodents leap through the rocks by the top of the ravine, challenging Tucker's marksmanship.

He raises his Smith & Wesson periodically at his prey, but with a wobbly gait and an unsteady hand he's overmatched and doesn't fire. Down the mountain they go, playing this humbling hunting game. "Fuck it," says Tucker after realizing the futility of it all. *My meal will have to wait, I'll save the bullets for Noodle.*

13

Ricky Salvador works high in the air in a safety harness hooked to a steel truss tower. A soldier in the Chilean army, Ricky prefers these riskier repair jobs over cleaning latrines any day. He's skilled with his hands, wielding wrenches and screwdrivers like a juggler wields flaming torches and swords. From up here, Ricky sees far beyond the electric fences of the Palma military outpost, out into the vast desert at the base of the grand Andes mountains.

In its heyday, Palma was a military outpost that housed a commando unit which combed the region for opponents of the Chilean military dictatorship. Only a skeleton crew supports the outpost now, to detect and limit the number of refugees who cross the desert after boating over the Pacific Ocean.

Strong winds batter Ricky on the tower, making repairs difficult. He attaches new housing for electronic equipment, tightening hexagonal screws with an array of Allen wrenches. Those winds are why Ricky's on the tower; the prevailing easterlies damage it all too frequently. His third time already this year, Ricky's become familiar with the tower, and he's respectfully named it the Steel Beast.

Ricky tightens the last of the screws and climbs down the Steel Beast. He unbuckles his harness and reaches into an ice chest with a beer that he's strategically placed. Ricky smiles back up at the Steel Beast, and toasts his acquaintance with an open beer, "Until next time my friend, until next time." He drains the beer and goes back to his barracks for a hot shower, content with a job well done. And now cell phone users in the Steal Beast's service area can be grateful.

14

By noon Esperanza has sent a text to Malcolm five times without success. Her condition has deteriorated and she's content to wait for him. The pain in her bloody swollen ankle is excruciating and she's fatigued and light-headed, classic signs of dehydration. Esperanza sends a text to Malcolm a sixth time.

Rudy, I see the desert. Attached is a picture. Can you locate me? Battery down to 25%. Thirsty and dizzy. Not walking well. Waiting here for you.

Bingo, the message goes through. An angel named Ricky Salvador looks over her.

15

Malcolm has walked for hours towards Esperanza's circle, her last known location. A Lonebud Police ballcap protects his head from the sun now beating down on him. He sips warm water from his half-full bottle, and checks his phone for his current location. Malcolm deduces that he's on track to bisect Esperanza's circle, like William Tell's arrow through the apple. Satisfied, he goes on.

He comes to a loma, a unique hill formation that collects fog from the Pacific Ocean. The loma has enough moisture for seasonal plants and a few animal species to thrive, an island of vegetation in an ocean of desert. Malcolm sees a flock of Andean flamingos eating algae, and a half mile further a South American gray fox eating a lizard.

The impromptu nature show ends abruptly when Malcolm feels a vibration in his pocket, the electromagnetic flare that Esperanza shoots through the air waves. Malcolm quickly grabs his phone and reads her text.

Rudy, I see the desert. Attached is a picture. Can you locate me? Battery down to 25%. Thirsty and dizzy. Not walking well. Waiting here for you.

His expression turns somber, and he regrets not having more water for her. Malcolm gets her current location from the ML4U website, surrounded by another circle with a 1/2-mile radius to reflect location accuracy. Esperanza has drifted southward. Malcolm decides to shift his course eastward, which he hopes will still put his arrow through the apple. He's only nine miles from her, and quite possibly from him. He taps the front pocket of his backpack and feels the hardness of his Glock pistol.

16

Eduardo leads the El Pulpo mule train, followed by Bernardo, Luta, Leti, and The Oz on Sylbuster. Leather satchels drape over the mules carrying essential supplies including food, water, sleeping bags, and tents.

They traverse up a series of narrow rocky switchbacks with breathtaking views of the Andes. Each rider clings to their sure-footed mule, instinctively tilting away from the edge of the mountain. "That's a long way down there," says The Oz nervously.

"And we have no parachutes," adds Luta.

"Oh relax ladies and enjoy the ride," says Eduardo who, like his brother, can speak English. "We're not going anywhere but up. We've got a job to do. Be alert for any signs of Esperanza or that nut job Miller."

Up they go without any further spoken word, except for the occasional, "good boy" directed at the beast between their legs. An hour later Eduardo pulls his reins and the mule train comes to an abrupt stop. "Lunch everyone," he commands.

The Oz dismounts Sylbuster gingerly. "Good, my crotch needs a break." He sits by Sylbuster on the switchback trail with a peanut butter and jelly sandwich. Luta and Leti sit next to The Oz and wedge tuna sandwiches into their mouths. Bernardo rubs his heavily bandaged leg, and reaches into the satchel draped over his mule and pulls out some goat stew.

Eduardo stands on the trail empty-handed, diligently scanning the mountain. "Nothing for you Dado?" says Bernardo.

"No way, I'm still a bit queasy."

El Pulpo enjoys a brief lunch. The men wrap it up by drinking water and stretching their limbs. They prepare to mount their mules when Eduardo, still on point, shields his eyes from the burgeoning sunshine and says, "Uh oh, looks like we've got company."

A trigger-happy Oz pulls out his Beretta. "Put that thing down," yells Eduardo. "It's only some goats." Eduardo sighs. "This ought to be interesting."

Indeed, when the goats arrive things get interesting. Or to be blunt, it's a cluster fuck of epic proportions. Scores of Boer and Nubian goats, herded by their elderly shepherd with a bushy gray beard and a wooden crook, are at an impasse with the El Pulpo mule train on the narrow rocky trail.

The mountainside comes alive with the din of goats bleating and mules braying. A few aggressive goats rear-up and feign head-butting with their horns. Some small rocks dislodge from the trail and fall off the mountainside into the abyss. The men of El Pulpo quickly grab the reins of their spooked mules before they can flee. A dust cloud of chaos forms. When it eventually starts to dissipate, the shepherd stomps forward and yells in Spanish, "Get out of my way, you're scaring my goats!"

"No old man," replies Leti in stilted Spanish, "you're in our way." All eyes turn to the inflammatory Leti.

Luta grabs Leti's arm. "Son, apologize to this man."

While Leti wriggles out of Luta's grasp, Bernardo intervenes, "We're sorry, he didn't mean it. Now stay calm and we'll figure out how to get you through."

The goats have already figured it out. They easily climb upslope and go around the El Pulpo blockade. The shepherd is not so agile though, and instead he carefully weaves through the men and mules of El Pulpo on the narrow rocky trail. He comes to the heavily bandaged Bernardo and eyes his wound. "Apology accepted. What happened to your leg?"

"We're policemen. I was shot. Maybe you can help us find the man who did this. He's out here somewhere."

"I haven't seen anyone. Not for three days. That's the beauty of shepherding."

"You haven't seen a woman either?"

"No, no one."

"Notice any signs of man? Smoke, noise, trash—"

"Noise. I heard a gunshot last night. I hear them occasionally. Didn't think much about it. Could that be your guy?"

"Maybe. Where'd the gunshot come from?" The shepherd points behind him. "Alright, thank you sir."

Most of the goats have returned to the switchback trail and the shepherd is anxious to join his herd. He steps past Bernardo and weaves through a final mule into the clear. Bernardo waves goodbye to the shepherd, but he's already guiding a stray Nubian with his crook and is oblivious to the salutation.

"Alright men, we're on the right track. Let's go," says Bernardo from his mule. The men pack trash, take final drinks of water, and mount their old mules. The El Pulpo mule train chugs along the switchback trail again, and once more Bernardo's leg jiggles and hurts. Bernardo fears the worst from the gunshot that the shepherd heard, and his stomach gurgles with goat stew.

17

The afternoon wears on and Esperanza's condition worsens. The swelling in her ankle has spread to her toes, which look like bratwurst, and dehydration ravages her body. Dizziness, lethargy, and thirst push her to the brink, and she senses the end. Esperanza calls Malcolm in desperation and, with her phone battery reading five percent, she knows this is her last flare. One ring . . . two rings . . . three rings . . .

The loma is far behind Malcolm, and he now navigates through a patch of thick brush. *Where's my damn machete?* he thinks. A branch scrapes his nose and he's Rudolph again. *Nice one moron.* Malcolm rests in the brush on the ground and enjoys the shade. He eyes his water bottle in the side pocket of his backpack and smacks his lips. *No, it's for Esperanza.* He grabs a granola bar from a box in the backpack. *Still plenty for her.*

One ring . . . Malcolm reaches into his front pants pocket but his phone's not there. Two rings . . . he hurriedly unzips the small middle pocket of his backpack but it's not there either. Three rings . . . he frantically unzips the main backpack compartment and scrambles madly through its contents. A ringing phone.

"Esperanza, can you hear me?"

"Rudy? My God, I got through."

Malcolm strains to understand. The reception is poor and, having a parched mouth, so is Esperanza's enunciation. "Hang in there Esperanza, I'm getting close. I can track this call and find you soon. I have food and water."

"I don't think I can walk anymore."

"Don't worry about it. I'll give you a piggyback."

"A piggyback? I'm a grown woman, are you sure you—"

Esperanza screams, a blood-curdling scream, and then a raspy male voice is on the line. "I'm sorry, my backstabbing daughter isn't available, can I take a message?" Tucker hangs up and laughs maniacally.

Malcolm has just received a knockout punch, a bone-jarring tackle, a fastball beaning, and it hurts. It hurts almost as much as when he got the tragic news about his wife and daughter. Esperanza is like a second daughter to him, even though he's only known her a short time.

Malcolm is devastated at the prospects for Esperanza, so he gets right to work. He visits the ML4U website once more and gets Esperanza's location during the ill-fated phone call. The boundary of her 1/2-mile-radius circle of accuracy is only a mile away. Malcolm jumps up, tosses his phone into his backpack, straps it on, and hurries away with renewed vigor. He enters the circle in minutes, a dangerous circle where estranged father and daughter await and, Malcolm fears, a violent resolution looms.

6

A CURIOUS PASTE

1

"You can have your phone back now," says Tucker. He throws it hard against a jagged andesitic rock, shattering Esperanza's lifeline. "Oops, a little too much mustard." Esperanza's heart races, her breathing quickens, and she cries tears of fear.

Tucker pokes at Esperanza's swollen bloody ankle with his cane and she cringes. "You're not going anywhere. And just to be sure . . ." He pulls out his Smith & Wesson and points it at Esperanza's head. "No, wait a minute." Tucker exchanges his gun for another one in the pockets beneath his wool poncho. "I think I like this one better. It's from the policeman I shot." Esperanza gasps. "Oh, did you know a policeman? Maybe someone who protected you from big bad daddy? Well, if it's any consolation, he was alive when I left him."

Tucker circles Esperanza with Bernardo's Colt pointed at her head. "We need to have a talk. Just me and you Noodle." The sun is low in the horizon. "It'll be dark soon. We're gonna need a fire to keep our chat warm and cozy. Why don't you get some rocks and make a fire ring?"

"I can't walk."

"Then crawl." Esperanza hesitates. "Go on." Her head fills with rage. *Asshole. A rapist, a murderer, and a real asshole.* She slowly combs the area on her knees and brings back three loads of andesitic rocks, including the one that destroyed her phone.

"Now go find some wood." *Asshole.* Esperanza crawls to a dead shrub and snaps off some branches. She slowly drags them back to the rocks on her knees. Tucker shakes his head at her haul. "A little short, don't ya think? You do want to have a warm and cozy chat, don't you?"

Esperanza's had enough. "Fuck you."

Tucker limps to Esperanza and presses the gun barrel against her temple. She grimaces and closes her eyes. After seconds that seem like minutes, Tucker lowers the gun. "We can't have a chat if your brains are splattered on the ground. I'll send you out for more wood later."

Tucker assembles the fire while Esperanza sits nearby rubbing her knees. He forms a ring with the rocks, and in it crumples scraps of paper from his wallet. He breaks up the dead shrub branches and sets them on the crumpled paper. A flick of his butane lighter ignites the paper and branches and sends sparks high into the sky.

"That's better," says Tucker as he holds his hands by the fire. "Now then, the last time we were together you slipped me a mickey and ran away. We had a good thing in that tunnel Noodle."

"Good for you, putting your hands on me, making me cook, making me clean. It was hell for me. For God's sake, I had to dump buckets of your shit! And my name is Esperanza. Your Noodle died when I left that tunnel."

"Perhaps I was a bit rough on you Noodle. And the touching, well, a man has needs. Outsmarting your old man and running away, I'll give you that one. Maybe it was time for you to get out into the world. The one I can't give you, the one that's getting you killed tonight is your blabbering to the police."

"Blabbering? What are you talking about?"

"The Bob's Beets case. Saw it on the news. They said a lady in Valvino, Chile told police she could identify a man in a tuna photo found at the Bob's Beets plant, and she was herself held captive by the man in Chile. A lady named Esperanza; you seem to fit the bill."

"I should've told them about you when I left that tunnel. Maybe those Bob's Beets girls would still be alive."

"Ah yes, the Bob's Beets girls. Seven of 'em I believe. Brenda was my favorite. She kept me happy for over four years with her 36Bs. Picked her up by offering her a free churro. Yeah, I had a nice gig there in Texas after you left the tunnel. Then of all the luck they demolish the plant. Somehow I make it out of there with just a bum hip. But my tuna photo didn't make it out. That damn tuna photo, and now you have cops around the world looking for me."

"And they'll find you."

"Maybe. They won't find you; I guarantee it."

"They know you killed mom and Billy."

"More of your blabbering? All the more reason to kill you. They can't prove it. Your mom had it coming, the nagging bitch. Billy was a handful with his autism, and he was draining us financially. He would've had a rough life too, so it was better to end it."

"You're so twisted."

"Maybe. You know what's twisted? That yellowfin tuna in the photo, I didn't catch it. A fishmonger was taking it to his market on the pier. Slipped him twenty bucks for the photo op. Makes for a good picture though, doesn't it?"

"You're pathetic. I should've known you didn't catch it. I loved that picture, 'til I hated it."

Tucker holds his hands by the fire. "Not puttin' out much heat anymore. I think it's time for some more wood now." Esperanza doesn't budge. "You know I could put a bullet in each of your fingers before I put one in your brain." Esperanza reluctantly crawls away to get more wood.

2

Walking at a frenetic pace, Malcolm suddenly stops to check his phone, and determines that he's near the center of Espernaza's circle. He pulls out his Glock and walks cautiously, surveying the landscape and looking for any sign of Esperanza and her crazed captor. The sky is turning dark, and something in the distance catches his eye. Malcolm stares through squinted eyes. He whispers, "Is that . . . yes . . . sparks!"

Like a lighthouse beacon, the sparks from Tucker's fire guide Malcolm. In minutes he's at the cusp of engagement. Malcolm hears voices now, and slows his gait to a crawl. He crouches behind some shrubs and parts the branches. Esperanza! And standing by her with gun in hand, Miller!

The fire has grown with the additional shrub branches that Esperanza dragged over on her knees. The glow illuminates Tucker like a spotlight as he delivers his sordid final act. "Thanks for the warm and cozy chat. It was nice catching up with you. But here's the deal, I can't risk having you testify against me. Maybe you deserve a better fate, but I can't give it to you. I can't give you a proper burial either without a shovel. Guess I'll have to leave you for the condors. They'll spread you around. It's the circle of life you know." Malcolm raises his Glock, poised to shoot.

3

Cy scans the darkening sky, and looks to the foothills in which Malcolm disappeared on his quest for Esperanza. "Where are they?" he mumbles. He turns his attention to his vintage yellow crop duster, carefully inspecting the propeller and wheels and slowly running his hands over the control surfaces. A cloud of dust catches his eye. "I'll be damned," he says.

The El Pulpo mule train slowly advances and kicks up dust. Eduardo's in front as before, and in minutes he's addressing Cy from his mule. "We're looking for a man and a woman."

"So am I. An old guy and his lady friend." Cy scratches his head. "They shoulda been here by now."

"What do you mean shoulda been here?"

"I flew the old guy out here. Goes by the name Malcolm. Says he's looking for his lady friend. I was gonna fly him and the girl back to Peralsco, but they shoulda been here by now."

The Oz perks up. "Malcolm? Malcolm O'Reilly?"

"Come to think of it, O'Reilly was his last name."

"He's a cop. Used to work at my police department. Maybe he found Esperanza."

"Or maybe Miller found her," says Eduardo ominously. "It's almost dark. Let's sleep here tonight and we can search for them first thing in the morning. Which way did Malcolm go?" Cy points to the northeast. "Alright then, tomorrow we make things right."

4

John Jordan was a bad man. His life of crime started at 11 with a candy shop break-in. He just had to have that rocky road fudge, a small treat to get him through another day with his abusive father. Henry Jordan regularly backhanded John, for not cleaning his room, or not scoring a goal in his soccer game, or not getting stellar grades at school. With unreasonable expectations and a dicey short temper, each day gave Henry a reason to hit John.

Soon John was doing the backhanding, to classmates, teammates, and stray dogs in the neighborhood. By his teens John was maiming or killing those stray dogs with his BB gun. When Henry was put away for assault, John moved-in with his alcoholic mother in Lonebud.

The streets of Lonebud were full of other troubled kids and they formed gangs. John joined the Westside Boys and assembled a long rap sheet, with his most serious crime being a burglary. While out on parole for the burglary, John needed some money for pot and held-up the Lonebud Savings and Loan. The armed robbery went badly and police responded to a silent alarm that the bank manager triggered. Malcolm was in the last patrol car to arrive at the scene, and joined a bevy of cops pointing their guns at John's head, who pointed his own gun at a female hostage.

John made a run for it with his screaming hostage and was hit with 12 bullets, including seven in the head. But one bullet also hit the hostage in the head, and the tragic standoff ended with two dead. The police inquiry never determined which cop shot the hostage, and Malcolm always wondered if it was him. Ever since that day he questions the use of lethal force, and gets a shaky trigger hand when he aims at someone's head.

With Esperanza's life in jeopardy, Malcolm aims at Tucker's head. A wave of uncertainty invades his body, and the characteristic shaky trigger hand manifests. He convinces himself that he can diffuse the situation with a disabling lower shot. Malcolm tilts the barrel of his Glock downward and his hand steadies. Slowly he squeezes the trigger and a 45-caliber bullet spins towards Tucker.

Tucker crumples to the ground and Bernardo's Colt bounces a few feet away. He writhes in pain from a gory bullet wound to his good leg. Coupled with his bad hip, Tucker isn't going anywhere. Esperanza seizes the opportunity. She crawls quickly over by Tucker and retrieves the Colt. Tucker overcomes his pain to pull out Eduardo's Colt from the cache of firearms in the pockets beneath his poncho. He points it at Esperanza, but Malcolm lodges a well-placed bullet into Tucker's gun hand and his thumb disintegrates. Tucker writhes again.

Esperanza looks around for the source of the gunshots and sees none. She hovers over Tucker on her knees, gun pointed between his eyes. She's dreamed of this moment for years and is overcome with emotion. She feels relief that Tucker will never again rape, murder, hurt, humiliate, irritate, or impart cruelty of any kind. But foremost she feels boundless anger for the man that destroyed much of her life. Now she can destroy his. Vengeance is sweet.

Tucker desperately pulls out his Smith & Wesson from the cache of firearms with his one functioning hand, his non-dominant left hand. The draw is slow and awkward, and Malcolm again lodges a well-placed bullet into Tucker's gun hand. Tucker writhes a third time, and with no useful limbs remaining he resembles a helpless bug kicking on its back. Esperanza inches the Colt closer to Tucker's face.

"You're not going to shoot me, are you Noodle?" says Tucker between groans.

Esperanza considers the question. "No." She lowers the gun.

"I didn't think you had it in you Noodle, to land a big one like me."

"My name is Esperanza. Let me hear you say it."

Tucker laughs, that evil maniacal laugh. Esperanza tosses the Colt aside and grabs a warm rock from the nearby fire ring, the jagged andesitic rock that destroyed her phone. She raises it overhead. The laughing ceases as Tucker sees rage building in Esperanza's face. Unbridled fear infuses his eyes, and Esperanza savors the look. "Let me hear you say my name."

"Noodle? You don't really—"

The cauldron boils over. Adrenaline is a powerful hormone, one that easily mitigates the devastating effects of dehydration. With a mighty cry and downward thrust of the rock, Esperanza squashes the bug. The rock crushes Tucker's face, emulating the sharp crack of a wood bat slugging a baseball. A startled Esperanza draws a deep breath as blood sprays onto her face and clothes. Seconds later she resumes the beating, a possessed rapid-fire forceful beating, one that she won't fully remember.

Tucker's head quickly becomes unrecognizable. His skull is in pieces, and gray brain matter mixes with blood to form a curious paste. Esperanza finally stops the beating, breathing hard and staring blankly at what used to be a man. Malcolm runs up to her and surveys the scene from a squat. Esperanza is calm and satisfied. Tucker is dead. When they embrace, Esperanza drops the rock onto the messy pile of bone and paste.

"Esperanza, are you alright?"

"I'm fine. He's done. It's over."

Malcolm wets a cloth with his water bottle and wipes away the blood on Esperanza's face. With each stroke he remembers wiping away his daughter's tears, after the cat scratched her, after her toy train broke, and after she couldn't get her sock off. Esperanza grabs the water bottle and chugs, letting out a satisfied sigh when finished. "Boy, did I need that," she says, and hands the water bottle back to Malcolm. She points to his red scraped nose. "You're Rudolph again."

"Another one of my moronic mishaps. Come on, let's get outta here. If you can stand for just a second, I'll get you on my back."

"But I'm too heavy, you can't—"

"I can. I just need to take some breaks on our way back. Let's go."

"Where are we going?"

"Well, I had a plane waiting for us in the desert, but the pilot should be taking-off before it gets too much darker. I'll make a call later and get us another plane for the morning."

Malcolm lifts Esperanza onto his back and takes a few steps. She looks back at the corpse. "What about him?"

"He goes to hell," says Malcolm emphatically. "Did you see the bottom of his boot? Looked like the Madonna. I think she would agree with me to send his sole there." Malcolm and Esperanza piggyback away, and a ravenous condor circles above Tucker's body.

5

With Esperanza on his back, Malcolm is slow and deliberate on the hike back to the desert, where Cy presumably has already lifted-off from the baked sand. He takes frequent breaks, gently setting Esperanza down and rationing himself to only three sips of water to conserve a dwindling supply. He feels the squeeze of Esperanza's arms around his neck, and is thankful to be going downhill under partial moonlight. Esperanza is exhausted and the rhythmic bobbing from Malcolm's steps drifts her close to sleep.

Malcolm passes the time with a conversation in his mind. *I haven't heard a plane. I wonder if Cy's still there. No, I told him to leave at dark. I'll call for another plane. I bet Pritchard can get me one. I hope I can get through to him. Keep going. One step at a time. Esperanza needs you. An ice-cold Imperial awaits. And a nice slab of ribeye.*

It's after midnight and Malcolm's back is on fire. His fingers won't uncurl after hours of holding Esperanza's legs and supporting her weight. And then his eyes fail him, or so he thinks. "Are you seeing this Esperanza?"

"I see it. Who are they? What are they doing?"

Malcolm and Esperanza overlook Cy and El Pulpo on the desert floor. They approach the group and see more details—five mules tied to the wheels and wings of the vintage yellow crop duster, the Delgado brothers sitting on a wing reading Cy's Playboy magazines by lantern light with heads canted and magazines rotated to view the centerfolds, The Oz and Leti playing catch with a rolled-up pair of socks, Luta playing ukulele sitting on a camp stool by a small fire, and Cy enjoying the music with another bottle of wine.

"That must be the trained task force that's trying to find you."

Esperanza cracks a smile. "No surprise they didn't."

Cy and the men of El Pulpo, except for Bernardo who's incapacitated, run to Malcolm and Esperanza when they reach the encampment. Malcolm gently lowers Esperanza to the ground a final time and rubs his aching back with the palms of his hands. The men are on high alert until Cy speaks. "You made it back, and with your lady friend."

"Better late than never," says Malcolm. "Am I glad to see you. I can't believe you're still here."

"Hell, I wasn't gonna leave ya."

The Oz goes to Esperanza to offer help, but mostly to flirt with the beautiful woman. "Are you alright miss?" He looks deep into her crystal blue eyes, hoping to cast his spell.

"Water, I need some more water. And a new ankle if you got one."

The Oz belts out a boisterous laugh, another element of his spell. "You must be Esperanza. I'm Ozwald Cosberg, but you can call me—"

"The Oz?" Esperanza looks at the front of his shirt.

"Why yes, The Oz." He flashes his best smile. "I'll get you that water now."

Malcolm straightens his aching back and addresses the group. "Gentlemen, I'm retired detective Malcolm O'Reilly and this is Esperanza Perez. I presume you're the task force sent to find her?"

"That's right," says Eduardo. "We call ourselves El Pulpo."

"Right." Malcolm has an agenda, and hearing more from Eduardo about El Pulpo isn't on it. "George Miller is dead. Our priority is to get Esperanza back home safely for medical treatment. As you can see, her ankle is in bad shape."

"And what's wrong with your fingers?" asks Cy.

"They're fine. Just locked up a bit." Malcolm pushes his fingers together and gradually straightens them. "See."

The Oz returns with a bottle of water. "Here ya go Esperanza."

"Thank you." She guzzles the entire bottle, spilling some water on the front of her red t-shirt. The Oz follows the drips.

Malcolm resumes. "We need to fly Esperanza back to Peralsco. Cy, when can you leave?"

"Checked out my duster already, she's ready to go."

"Good. Let's get you going ASAP. I'll stay here and leave with El Pulpo in the morning. I can double-up with someone on one of the mules."

"Alright, now that we have a plan let's celebrate," says Cy. He holds out his bottle of wine to Malcolm and Esperanza. "Can I pour you some?"

Wanting only water, they shake their heads. Malcolm also shakes in disgust and challenges Cy, "What happened to eight hours between bottle and throttle?"

"Do I look like a commercial airline pilot? Relax, I got ya here, didn't I?"

"You can pour me some more," says Luta. He holds out his cup and Cy fills it. After a healthy swig, Luta plucks *What a Wonderful World* on the ukulele. His audience enjoys the song, but Malcolm grows impatient. Luta finally brings it home, "Yes I think to myself, what a wonderful world." A polite smattering of applause fills the desert air.

"That was nice," says Malcolm. "Maybe we can hear more after we get Cy and Esperanza airborne. Let's get these mules unhitched."

Minutes later Luta and Leti hold the reins of the mules, standing way back from the crop duster. Eduardo stands by them with his arm around his gimpy brother. Cy is in the cockpit adjusting his single-lensed goggles, ready to go. The Oz lifts Esperanza onto the wing of the plane, easily the strongest and most qualified man for the job. Malcolm embraces her on the wing. "You're gonna be fine. I'll check on you before I head back to Costa Rica. Bye Esperanza." He plants a kiss on her head.

"Bye Rudy. I can't thank you enough. I owe you my life. And I owe you a backrub."

"I'll take one of those," interjects The Oz. Malcolm and Esperanza part and The Oz lifts Esperanza into the backseat.

"Or maybe I can buy you a cup of coffee after we get back to Valvino." The Oz actually bats his eyes.

"We'll see . . . Oz."

"Here, put these on," says Cy who hands Esperanza a pair of goggles. "Okay, everybody back, I'm gonna start 'er up." Cy checks the area by the propeller. "Clear," he yells and then the engine belches a puff of black smoke and the propeller turns. The engine noise scares the mules, and Luta and Leti struggle to restrain them. The plane rolls forward and Cy and Esperanza wave goodbye. They speed across the desert and into the night air, enveloped by the cloak of darkness.

"Well that's it then," says Malcolm. "How about another one of your tunes?" Luta grabs his ukulele and plucks a few notes before a familiar noise drowns out his song. Cy buzzes by at full throttle not 50 feet off the ground and wags his wings. Malcolm smiles. "Crazy bastard."

6

A beautiful cloudless morning breaks and El Pulpo is packed for the long journey back over the Andes to Valvino. They leave no trace of their overnight stay in the desert, except for mule poop which dots the baked sand. Eduardo leads the mule train once again, with Malcolm doubled-up with The Oz on Sylbuster at the rear. The Oz grips the reins tightly, still terrified of the beast between his legs. Malcolm awkwardly holds on to The Oz from behind, bombarded by "The Coz" on the back of his shirt.

"We have a lot to talk about," says The Oz as the mule train departs. "You do know that I have your old detective position at the Lonebud police force, don't you?"

"I had no idea. So you're the one who . . . who has my spot. Pritchard must've sent you here. How the hell is he?"

"As crotchety as ever."

"Jesus Christ!"

"Excuse me?"

"Those thorns in the back of your head. You look like Jesus Christ."

"Oh yeah, I must've missed a few. Sylbuster here took me for a ride through a thorn bush. The damn thing has a mind of its own. Doesn't seem to know what a rein is." Malcolm laughs and gives Sylbuster an appreciative pat on the rear as he marches on to the Andes.

7

Esperanza rests comfortably in her Valvino cabin. Her ankle shows no signs of infection after taking antibiotics, and the swelling is gone in a few weeks. But a nasty serpentine scar remains following the removal of 11 stitches, as well as the mental scar of yet another traumatic event in her life.

Piles of new wall hangings, beaded pouches, ponchos, and hats with earflaps and tassels rest in a corner of her cabin. Esperanza puts the finishing touches on a special hat that she's been working on, and places it in one of the piles. Recuperation gives her a chance to knit and weave all day, reflect on her life, and weigh her options. She wonders again if there's more to life than knitting and weaving.

Esperanza can walk normally again following an extended recuperation. Today she walks through her pearl town, breathing harder than usual in the altitude after nearly a month of inactivity. Snow sprinkles into her face with the push of a light headwind. She stops at the bank to get money, at a flower shop to buy a bouquet of red roses, at the internet café to catch up on world news, and at the Café Cabra for a terrific lunch plate of bean stew.

After lunch Esperanza walks to the grave of her dear friend Paola Ramos. She runs into the young boy with a club foot selling Chiclets and buys a couple of boxes. They consummate the deal with smiles and a big hug. At the cemetery Esperanza lays the bouquet of red roses by Paola's headstone and removes the bouquet of Sacred Flowers of the Andes that she left weeks ago, now wilted and dusted with snow. She says a prayer and wipes a tear from her eye.

Her final stop is at the patchy field near the central plaza to watch the kids play soccer. An errant kick sends the worn-out ball out of bounds right to her. A boy with silky black hair and crystal blue eyes, just like hers, comes to retrieve the ball. They lock eyes and smile, and Esperanza hands him the ball. She leaves with the usual smile on her face, but also with tears in her eyes, for she longs to know this boy and yet knows she must not know him.

8

Malcolm reclines in a blue-striped beach chair under a large matching umbrella, drinking an ice-cold Imperial at his favorite Costa Rican beach after a game of fetch with his golden retriever, Gemini. Gemini is out exploring, and Malcolm expects her back soon. Through sunglasses he watches for Gemini, and watches the powerful ocean waves break. He listens to the crash of the surf and the squawk of the seagulls, and inhales the invigorating salt air. A distant container ship floats on the horizon, and then suddenly it's gone, concealed by a beautiful dark-haired woman with a familiar face.

"Hello Rudy," says Esperanza with a huge smile.

"My God, you came! After I saw you all bandaged-up in Valvino, I didn't think I'd be seeing you for a while."

"You know how much I've wanted to visit you and the beaches, and I've been thinking maybe I don't want to knit and weave the rest of my life. I thought maybe I could stay here a while and help you take care of things. This is the best place for me to clear my head, so here I am."

"Of course you can stay here. I can't think of anyone else I'd rather have. I could use the company, and the help. It's almost time to harvest my guava tree."

"Thank you." She gives him a peck on the head and reaches into her backpack. "I made something for you." She hands him a white wool hat with earflaps and tassels, inscribed with "Rudy" in bright red.

"I love it." Malcolm puts it on. "This will keep the rain and sun off my head. I don't know if I'll ever take it off."

"I have a feeling it'll come off on hot days." Esperanza kneels down beside Malcolm. The warm sand feels good on her knees. "I owe you a backrub, remember?"

"How could I forget? Tell you what, you can take me to Julia, the best masseuse in town. I'm rubber after she's through with me." Malcolm lays down a beach towel for Esperanza on the sand next to his chair. She sits on it while he reaches into an ice chest.

"You must be hungry. Here, try this." Malcolm offers her some cantaloupe. As Esperanza chews on a piece she reflects on how grateful she is for all this man has done for her—helping her find evidence at that awful tunnel, tracking her down with a madman on the loose, saving her life with precision gunshots, carrying her to safety on his back for miles, and now letting her stay with him in paradise.

"Wow, that's good."

"I grow it in my garden. I grow cherimoya too. Isn't that your favorite?"

"I love cherimoya. In Spanish it's 'chirimoya.' How's your Spanish coming along?"

"Bueno." Malcolm searches for words and slowly finds them. "Bienvenido a Costa Rica. Parece que has encontrado tu playa."

"Very good. 'Welcome to Costa Rica. Looks like you've found your beach.' I have found my beach. And a dear friend . . . who's like a father to me."

Suddenly Gemini returns wet, sandy, panting, and with tail wagging wildly. She finds her slobbery fetching ball under Malcolm's chair and mouths it. "I guess we're playing fetch again," says Malcolm. "Why don't you throw it to her?"

"I can't throw, remember?"

"I remember showing you how to cast a fly-fishing rod. Throwing a ball's the same thing. Go on, try it. Gemini's waiting."

Esperanza pries the ball from Gemini's mouth and throws a good one down the beach. Gemini retrieves it for Esperanza, kicking up powdery white sand each way. They play a few minutes, with Esperanza having almost as much fun as Gemini. Malcolm cherishes the scene and laughs. "Now throw one to me," he says still wearing his wool hat. Esperanza fires a perfect strike from 50 feet. "That's my girl." Malcolm smiles. "That's my girl."

Also by Bruce Shaffer

It Started with a Pickle Crock
The Bonnacon Goes to Calgary
The Bonnacon Goes to Pamplona
The Final Play
A Goat's Life
The Folsom Rewind

www.ingramcontent.com/pod-product-compliance
Lightning Source LLC
Chambersburg PA
CBHW021539150726
47990CB00006B/2319